Knock-knock-knock

Also by E. Lowri

In the Stick of Time
The Stocking Filler
Reticent Road

Did Someone Knock?

E. LOWRI

e-lowri.com

Copyright © E. Lowri 2024

The right of E Lowri to be identified as the author of this has been asserted by her in accordance with the Copyright, Designs and Patents Act 1988

This is a work of fiction. Names, characters, places, and incidents either are the product of the author's imagination or are used fictitiously. Any resemblance to actual persons, living or dead, events, or locales is entirely coincidental

All rights reserved. No part of this book may be reproduced or used in any manner without written permission of the copyright owner except for the use of quotations in a book review

ISBN: 9798341432628

First edition

Independently published.

With a swipe of the hand, fate can alter our life as quickly as it can extinguish it.

Make friends with fate.

Chapter 1   9
Strangers on a Platform

Chapter 2   26
The King's Feet

Chapter 3   45
A Stranger's Passing

Chapter 4   57
Alone Together

Chapter 5   70
Trust all but No One

Chapter 6   82
Scattered Seeds

Chapter 7   97
Smoky Fish

Chapter 8   112
Beginning of the End

Chapter 9   127
The Mask

Chapter 10   139
The Murderer Among Us

Chapter 11   150
From Bar to Bars

Chapter 12   163
End Scene

Chapter 1
Strangers on a Platform

"Fate decides what humans cannot."

The infamous face of the menacing man smiles eerily at Otis; the scar down the man's cheek fractures whenever he breaks into his signature Cheshire Cat grin. Otis watches on, helpless, as the man turns and walks away from him. Otis calls out, ordering him to return. He shouts until his lungs throb. He tries to tell his colleagues that they need, *must*, prevent this man from leaving; he is a threat to society, Otis insists. *A murderer*. It is all in vain though; his colleagues merely stand there, staring at Otis with emotionless expressions as if he is some sort of lunatic. The loud thud of a gavil rings out.

'Silence', the booming voice of the judge demands.

Unpeaceful silence falls. One by one his colleagues turn away and disappear out through the door. The last colleague hesitates and looks back towards Otis, their eyes fill with disappointment. The colleague sighs and turns the lights off as he exits, leaving Otis standing alone in the darkness. He feels something touch his arm, and looks down to find *the* child tugging gently on his sleeve.

'You let him get away', the child says, her grieving eyes stare into his.

Otis is awoken from this nightmare by the sound of the train steward making an unexpected announcement. He can feel his heart racing, pounding unrhythmically. It was the same old dream, unrelenting in its quest to conquer his unconscious. He looks around, no one has noticed him. *Good*, he thinks, relieved that he must not have screamed out this time.

A lanky looking young man with jumbled hair is stood talking on the phone in the gangway; he pauses his call and pokes his head through the carriage door, as the train speakers crackle into life:

'We are sorry to announce that due to stormy weather near Hammersly, resulting in debris on the track up ahead, we will be terminating this journey at Dillingford Station. We apologise for any inconvenience. Please ensure you disembark the train at the next stop and take all belongings with you. We're working with Calnesbury bus company to arrange a service to take you from Dillingford station to Hammersley, as soon as possible.'

Otis glances at his fellow passengers, there is barely anyone left on this two-carriage train. The lanky man continues to hover, as if anticipating a further update. His fair complexation suggests his black hair is not its true shade, and his eyes are wide and alert; they are quite striking owing to their vivid blue colour.

A woman sits adjacent to Otis on the other side of the aisle. She looks unnerved by the premature end of the train ride. She clutches a mystery novel close to her chest. Otis's eyes linger a little longer on her than he intended; she spots him, he immediately looks away and smiles. Wrong order, Otis thinks, annoyed that he smiled at the ceiling instead of the woman. Her spectacles appear to magnify her green hued eyes, that sparkle like diamonds under the train lights.

A sharp bang is suddenly heard from the rear of the carriage, caused by another young man thumping the table in front of him with his fist. Otis studies the lime green hoodie the young man is wearing; written across it are the words: Only Yoda Knows. The hooded man looks shrouded with anger. *He certainly doesn't channel Yoda*, Otis thinks. The man pulls back his green hood, revealing thick locks of hair; he scratches his beard due to frustration at the situation, rather than necessity.

A scruffy looking attendant walks briskly through the carriage keeping his head down, no doubt in a bid to avoid any confrontational customers.

'Can't you do something? I can't just be plonked at a random station. I'm meant to be in Hammersley for a connecting train', the hooded man fumes.

'No, disembark at Dillingford. You'll get to Hammersley eventually', the attendant says abruptly, before continuing his march to the front of the train.

'I've never even heard of Dillingford', the woman says forlornly.

The attendant rushes past her, choosing to ignore her remark.

A fourth person appears to be slumped, possibly still asleep, right at the back of the carriage. Otis cannot make out much more than the outline of the limp-looking figure.

'What the hell!?', the slumped man cries, rubbing sleep from his eyes.

The slumped man stares up at the news of their fate, that now garishly flashes in bright orange letters on the electronic sign overhead. There is something old-fashioned about him, Otis thinks, admiring his tweed ensemble as he watches the man stand up and look around the carriage in bewilderment.

The lanky man hovering in the doorway, still clutching his phone to his chest, tuts and rolls his eyes dramatically.

'Seems like all of us were heading for Hammersley then?', the lanky man declares.

Everyone looks around at one another, speaking no words but awkwardly nodding in agreement.

'Bloody brilliant', the lanky man mutters grumpily.

Glancing down at his phone, he quickly returns to the space between the carriages to continue his phone call. Otis cannot hear what is being said but he watches the lanky man for a moment, pacing and talking quickly. Otis assumes he is frantically trying to rejig his now derailed plans.

The hooded man disappears into the toilet cubicle at the very back of the train, passing the tweed-cladded man, who remains standing and busily flicking through his phone. The woman near Otis retreats into the pages of her book.

'Excuse me? Do you know where Dillingford is in relation to Hammersley? The internet on my phone is very slow', the tweed-cladded man asks Otis, appearing next to him.

Otis pulls out his phone and opens the map; it loads partially but not enough to see exactly where they are.

'Mine is pretty slow too I'm afraid', Otis says.

'Thanks for trying', the tweed-cladded man says glumly.

'I'm not overly familiar with the area but my guess would be it's about an hour away, based on when we were meant to be arriving in Hammersley', Otis says, trying to be as helpful as he can.

The man thanks him again, and slowly heads back to his seat. Otis detects an aura of sadness surrounding the tweeded man; he finds himself feeling a little sorry for him. He looks like a man who is a step out of time from everyone else. The train suddenly enters a tunnel, causing a couple of the top windows to slam shut. The woman gasps, and quickly looks embarrassed by her unnecessary jumpiness. Unable to continue reading her book, she seems unsure what to do with herself.

As the train emerges from the confines of the tunnel, the hooded man re-appears looking increasingly vexed.

'Stupid thing!', the man cries.

Otis looks behind him, the hooded man appears to be having trouble with his phone. He holds down the button on the side of the device.

'Ah yes, the old turn it off and on-again trick. The last act of a desperate man', Otis muses quietly to himself.

The lanky man wears the same pained expression as he taps at his phone, his call seemingly unexpectedly ended. Otis looks down at his own device; he has lost signal too. The lanky man returns to his seat, huffing and puffing as he plonks himself down like a ragdoll.

'Unbelievable. Bloody Dillingford', the lanky man says, followed by a loud tut of the tongue.

Otis senses the man is deliberately putting on a rather theatrical show for attention. He tuts some more in case Otis was in any doubt.

Otis looks outside and eyes with trepidation the dark clouds that lie up ahead. As the train steadily slows, he has a rising resentment over Britain's inability to deal with any kind of adverse weather. The sun is setting rapidly, and little life can be seen as the train moves closer to their destination. Otis leans back in his seat, enjoying the last moments in the warmth of the train. Reaching into his pocket he pulls out an envelope; inside it is a scribbled note that reads:

21 Western Way, Hammersley. Last known address of his sister. She used to work at Harold's News – old newsagents on Roderick Road.

Otis puts the note back in his pocket. *Am I doing the right thing?*, he thinks. The legal way of dealing with the man in the nightmare had not worked. Despite the man's guilt, he walks free as an innocent man. Otis continues to suppress his better judgement, determined to pursue a less legal way to secure justice. The anger from all those months ago, when the verdict was read, clings to him like a parasite. He wishes it would release its grip on him, but it never does.

The train comes to a halt at the unwanted stop. The passengers obediently, and rather gloomily, begin to depart. Otis allows the four other passengers to exit before he reaches for his battered-looking leather satchel, and heads for the open door. He is greeted by an unloved looking sign:

Welcome to Dillingford Station

A solitary spotlight shines down on the group of five strangers, who are all stood stiffly in a line a few feet apart from each other. Otis assumes that out in the surrounding darkness of nightfall, is nothing but a mass of rolling fields. It is a twee village station, that looks as if it has not changed since it was built in the 1920s. A tiny square ticket booth is positioned at the entrance; the small hatch is bolted shut, and only looks big enough to seat one person when open. The thick cobwebs and rusted hinges give the impression it is no longer used.

The dishevelled looking attendant leans out of the train door.

'A minibus has been arranged to come and collect you and take you to Hammersly. It'll be here within the hour', he says gruffly, before promptly shutting the door.

The train hisses and creeks, as it begins to edge away from the station heading back the way it came.

'They should have let us sit on the train until the bus arrived', says the hooded man, his cheeks flush with agitation.

He proceeds to jab at his phone frantically. Otis watches him persist in his doomed quest to magic up some signal.

'Nothing!', the hooded man cries. 'No network. No public internet. What a joke.'

'I didn't even know there was a station here', the woman says with a bewildered look on her face, as she surveys the tiny platform.

Otis spots a long bench under a shelter and heads towards it; the four fellow passengers follow him like a line of lost ducklings. They each perch on the bench. The atmosphere is tense. Everyone clutches a phone and mindlessly stares at it, unsure what to do with the device when it is unable to connect to the world, and they appear unable to connect with each other.

'This is stupid, they can fly people into space but can't ensure the whole of the country gets signal or Wi-Fi', the hooded man groans.

No one replies but Otis senses a mutual agreement between them.

'It does feel a tad primitive to leave us at the mercy of a bus, with no way to contact anyone', the tweed-cladded man says.

Everyone agrees; it is a situation that no one expects to find themselves in these days.

'The latest phones designed by Evolution and ModTech will allow you to make calls to emergency services via satellite', the hooded man says.

He stares at his own phone with derision.

'Fat lot of good that will do us though. They come out tomorrow', he adds.

Otis cannot help but chuckle.

The minutes tick by painfully slowly. Few words are spoken. The sound of hooting owls and fox cries occasionally breaks the silence.

'Always sounds like a woman being murdered to me, whenever a fox starts screaming at night', the woman says thoughtfully.

Meant as a light-hearted interlude, the woman senses it was not the most reassuring thought to place in people's minds right now. Otis notices everyone's body tense. The thunder rumbling in the distance also serves to keep everyone on edge. Otis had already spotted multiple cracks in the shelter, rendering it useless should the storm come this way. He traces the cracks in his leather satchel with his finger; this bag had become like a comfort blanket to him. Each line he traced represented some battle he had fought; some case he had solved. He twizzles the loose button on the satchel; that, however, represents a case he never closed. Shutting his eyes for a moment he is taken back to his old Police Station: *shut in a room with his superior he had swung the bag in a rage against the wall, inadvertently catching the button on the back of a chair. 'You need to calm down', his superior had said.* He re-opens his eyes. The woman glances over at him; she detects all is not calm in his mind.

As they reach the 59th minute the hooded man, who had remained glued to his useless phone, hysterically declares that the bus is not coming.

'Well, that's it then, isn't it? We're going to end up getting caught in the storm with nowhere to go, no one to save us. I mean, look around – where the hell are we?', the hooded man cries.

Otis suspects he is correct about the bus never coming. British transport is not something he would ever bet his life on. Otis reckons that somewhere, right now, there is a bus driver completely oblivious that he is meant to be the salvation for a group of people stranded in Dillingford.

'A village will be nearby', Otis says calmly, glancing down at his own signal-less phone: 9.02pm the clock reads.

'Better to remain together and use the torch lights from our phones to navigate the lanes. There'll be a local pub we can call into, I'm sure', Otis says, glancing at the flustered, hooded man.

'I'm Otis, what's your name?', he asks.

The hooded man looks startled and takes a few moments to decide if it is safe to reveal such a detail to a group of strangers.

'Er...Muhsen', he replies.

Otis smiles reassuringly. Muhsen appears to be the most apprehensive of them all. Otis looks around at the other faces, a mix of nerves and annoyance fills their eyes.

'I'm Daphne', the woman announces quietly, using her glasses as a shield, clutching them tightly with her hand.

'Kiki', the tweed-cladded man says with a cheeky grin. 'It was my mother's idea to name me that, not mine', he adds.

Everyone turns to the final stranger. A man dressed from head to toe in knock-off designer gear. The lanky, tutting man. A man that emanates fake confidence.

'I am sure I don't need to introduce myself. I am Jefferson Riley.'

Everyone stares at him blankly.

'Don't be starstruck, we A-class influencers are mere mortals like you', he continues, with a forced smile.

Everyone remains as flummoxed as they had been seconds ago. Clearly no one had heard of him, a fact that Jefferson chooses to ignore.

'Right, well', Otis says shifting the subject. 'Let's get going, in case the storm is heading our way. Everyone, turn your phone lights on, and let's remain close to ensure we are all seen should any cars appear.'

'Um... I... I'm afraid my phone has no light', says Daphne.

She holds up a phone that Otis has not seen for decades.

'Goodness! Those things are in museums now', he says, smiling.

Daphne looks sheepish.

'I've never been one for modern tech', she replies.

Muhsen stares at the brick-like device like it is some sort of primitive alien technology.

'What's even the point of that? You must only be able to see a couple of words at a time on that screen, and just a tiny fragment of a website', Muhsen says.

'Oh, you can't go on the internet or anything. Just text and call', Daphne replies.

Muhsen audibly gasps, he looks like he has received the most shocking news of his life.

'You don't know what you're missing out on', Jefferson says cockily, brushing his hand through his windswept hair.

Everyone knew he was referring to his own social media presence.

'Yet somehow I've survived', Daphne replies with a sarcastic undertone.

'Right come on, let's go', Otis says authoritatively, not wishing to waste any more time, sensing an imminent storm.

'Wait', says Jefferson. 'My offline map tells me that Dillingford is about three or four miles up that way but there is a pub called The King's Feet on route, about one mile away.'

'The King's Feet?', Otis says bemused. 'Are you sure it's not Arms?'

'If I had Wi-Fi I'd be able to tell you exactly why it's called that', Muhsen interjects grumpily. 'I can't even view the maps offline, what a joke.'

'Well at least we know a landlord-cum-comedian awaits us', says Otis.

Jefferson rolls his eyes as if such humour is beneath him. Daphne smiles at Otis, appreciating the level-head among them.

The group of strangers begin walking, huddled together like a newly formed pack. Their phone lights allow them to see only ten feet or so ahead. The starless sky and hidden moon make the darkness suffocating. Daphne, the only one without a light of her own, darts her head around like a startled owl; convinced they are being followed.

'It's only because you can't see behind you, it makes your imagination go into overdrive and think something could be there', Kiki says to Daphne.

Daphne nods before glancing behind her again. Every so often a cool breeze whips around their exposed hands and faces, sending a chill through their bodies.

'So, what do you do?', Daphne asks Kiki, wishing for a further distraction.

'I'm a poet', Kiki says proudly.

Jefferson lets out a snort.

'I'm sure that comes with hefty earnings', Jefferson says coolly.

Daphne shakes her head.

'Ignore him', she says.

Kiki leans towards Daphne.

'Well, I do have a job as a part-time barista to pay the bills', he says.

Daphne smiles.

'I can't stand all this fake AI, social media nonsense. Nothing is genuine anymore. That's why I cling to the written word; crafted by the hand of human emotion, rather than a programmed computer,' Kiki says.

'I understand', Daphne replies, feeling slightly enamoured of Kiki's way of thinking.

She cannot quite see Jefferson's face, but she would guess he looks perturbed by these comments. Sure enough, it is not long before Jefferson breaks the silence.

'I think you need to move with the times. Or else, just get left behind', Jefferson says.

'Well, I guess I'll just get left behind then. Sounds bliss to me', Kiki retorts.

Jefferson does not respond; Daphne concludes it is because he is unable to think of a good comeback.

'Do you live in Hammersley, or are you heading there for a visit?', Daphne says, returning to her conversation with Kiki.

'We poets go wherever the road takes us', Kiki declares whimsically.

'So, a visit then', Muhsen mutters.

Daphne finds the whole ensemble comical; a cast of misfits thrown together by some leaves on a train track.

'Oh, how much longer?', Jefferson demands.

'Well, let's see. Given we have only been walking for five minutes, a little bit longer', Otis snaps.

'I'm definitely going to film a strongly worded vlog when we reach the pub', says Jefferson. 'My fans would probably organise a rescue mission if they knew'.

The arrogance that oozes from him is almost more than Otis can tolerate.

'Fans or followers?', Kiki asks.

'Same thing', Jefferson says.

Kiki smirks.

'I don't think it is', he replies, much to Jefferson's surprise.

'What do you mean by that?', he asks Kiki.

The imminent debate is abruptly interrupted by Daphne.

'Look over there, headlights', she says, looking behind her.

They all come to a halt, staring at the moving headlights approaching in the distance.

'Let's hope it's the minibus', Kiki says.

'It's approaching pretty fast', Jefferson says with increasing alarm.

'Quick move to the side of the road!', Otis cries.

The squeal of fast-moving wheels echoes in the darkness, as the vehicle rounds the corner.

'STOP!', Jefferson shouts waving his arms around.

The car pays no attention and zooms past them causing specs of dust and dirt to fly into their faces. For the first time, Daphne is actually thankful to wear glasses.

'Bastard!', Jefferson calls out.

The car suddenly comes to a halt; the red of the brake lights illuminate the road. Otis struggles to make out what type of car it is, except that it is red and sporty. It moved too fast to see the identity of the driver.

'Now you've done it, Jefferson', Muhsen says. 'Pissed off a maniac whilst we're trapped in the middle of nowhere.'

Jefferson does a signature tut. Otis feels like putting tape over his mouth if he tuts again. *No just breathe,* Otis tells himself. They all watch the car closely. The brake lights tap on and off.

'Oi!', Jefferson shouts.

'We're all stuck here. Help us, would you?', he continues.

Otis feels Jefferson's tone could have been a little friendlier; the driver appears to agree. The car speeds off down the road in the direction of the village.

'Well, that was a bit strange', Daphne says once the car is out of sight.

Otis nods in agreement, giving a resentful glance towards Jefferson.

'Just some idiot who fancies themselves invincible, based on their driving skills', Kiki says with a slight shakiness in his voice, clearly feeling unnerved.

'He could have helped us. Not as if this is a main road with lots of people around', Jefferson says.

'Perhaps that's why they didn't. I mean, not sure I would pick up five strangers in the middle of nowhere', Daphne replies.

They continue to make their way down the country lane, encountering no other vehicle on their journey. The trek feels all the more daunting due to their limited vision; every minute that passes seems to drag on a little longer than the last. Even Otis has to admit this feels like the longest walk he has ever done. Very little is said between the strangers, the situation does little to invite small talk.

'Over there! Looks like the faint light of the pub', Daphne says, pointing in the distance.

'Not exactly the dazzling lights of London, is it?', Jefferson says.

'What do you expect? We're in the middle of bloody nowhere', Muhsen scoffs.

'He's a laugh, isn't he?', Jefferson says to Otis.

Otis does not respond, keeping his eyes focussed on the destination ahead. The sight of salvation gives everyone a burst of energy; the pace picks up. Muhsen looks at his phone once again, increasingly perturbed that there is still no signal.

'The last couple of hours has felt like the start of an old-fashioned horror story', Daphne says. 'Stranded with strangers, no way of contacting the outside world'.

Otis knew Daphne's remark was meant to be humorous, but it seems to send a shiver through everyone's spine.

'Well, obviously we are not in a horror story', Daphne adds, regretting her choice of words once again.

'Depends on what horrifies you; it is all relative. Personally, I can't think of anything worse than being stuck with total strangers in the middle of nowhere, and no way to contact friends or family', Muhsen says.

'I actually love a good, spooky mystery. Well, reading one. Not sure about being part of one', Daphne says.

A sudden burst of thunder makes everyone jump.

'This certainly seems like a solid start to some sort of spooky mystery' though, Daphne says, with a weak laugh.

'Nah, this is all too stereotypical. Darkness, thunder, isolated strangers', Kiki says, waving his hand dismissively.

'But why do you think so many mysteries have this kind of setting? It's because the devils among us know this is an ideal backdrop to carry out their deeds,' Daphne says.

No one responds. Everyone waits for someone else to say something.

'Blimey, you've got a morbid side, haven't you?', Kiki says to Daphne, light heartedly.

Daphne launches into a wheezy laugh, causing her to cough.

'No, no. I enjoy reading lots of mystery novels, that's all', Daphne replies.

'Well then, Kiki, I am expecting your poems to contain no such stereotypes, although I won't hold my breath', Jefferson says.

Kiki manages to hold his tongue, despite finding Jefferson one of the most irritating people he has met. Daphne and Kiki exchange a look that conveys an equal dislike for Jefferson. She cannot understand how he could possibly influence anyone, at least not in a positive way.

'What exactly do you vlog about?', Kiki asks Jefferson.

Daphne is sure she hears a groan from Otis, no doubt dreading the monologue that is about to follow.

'Life and death', Jefferson says flippantly.

No-one immediately responds. Otis believes everyone is waiting for more information, but Jefferson appears remarkably lacking in words.

'Bit broad', Kiki says finally.

'What else is there to vlog about?', Jefferson says.

Kiki finds his answers odd. This was Jefferson's moment to brag, yet he seems to have squandered the chance on vague answers. Otis knows nothing of the world of influencers, nor does he wish too. He does wonder how much of a successful influencer Jefferson really is though.

As they round the corner to the entrance of the pub, Otis has a heavy feeling in the pit of his stomach; he is unsure why. A sign flaps in the wind, with a faint light above it; a useless light that is not even bright enough to read the sign. As they reach the front it seems very quiet, and a little rundown. Made from classic grey stone, Otis has no doubt that in the light of day it is a striking building, against the backdrop of the sublime British countryside. The large front door has a unique iron knocker in the shape of a wolf's head; its eyes give the impression they follow you wherever you go.

'Don't be fooled, these local pubs may look worse for wear, but it'll be brimming with locals inside. After all, it's the only place around for miles', Kiki says, rubbing his hands together in anticipation.

Aside from the rustling trees there is no sign of life anywhere beyond the pub walls. The whole place is enveloped in darkness, making it difficult to get a true feel for the surroundings. Otis casts his eyes around; he hopes there is a car park at the back brimming with the vehicles of friendly regulars. Daphne is still unable to shake the sense they are being watched.

The curtains at the front are partially drawn, making it difficult to see what awaits them within.

'Is it even open?', Muhsen says, studying the unimpressive facade.

'Only one way to find out', Otis says.

The group burst through the door of the quaint pub hoping to be greeted by a bustling crowd of local drinkers. Much to their disappointment the pub is empty. A lone lady stands behind the bar and looks as surprised to see them, as they are to see her standing alone.

'Wow. A rush! Don't think I have ever experienced that here', the landlady says.

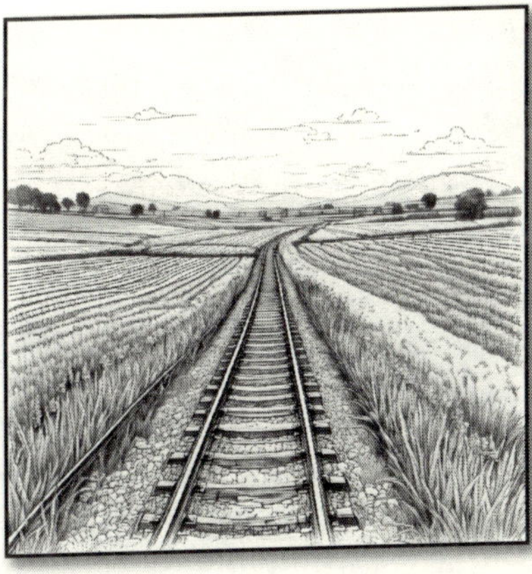

Chapter 2
The King's Feet

"The smallest of lights brings hope, to the weariest of travellers."

The group of strangers remain huddled together near the entrance. There is an empty charm to the pub; the place feels like it was once handsome but now what remains is a hollowed-out shell. To the right of the entrance is a larger L-shaped seating area, with a mix of tables and booths. Generic artwork adorns the walls, and random figurines of hares and foxes are dotted around the place. The lighting is dim, giving it an old-worldly feel. To the left of the bar is a further seating area with armchairs and sofas, and an impressive stone fireplace. Large, square pillars are dotted throughout making it hard to get a clear view; these appear to be decorative rather than functional. It is an unusual look but somehow works. Otis steps out ahead of the group.

'We've walked from the station, our train got cancelled. We don't seem able to get network on our phones, could we use your phone by any chance? Or Wi-Fi?', Otis asks.

'Before you get into that, could you show me where the loos are? I've had three espressos before getting on the train', Jefferson says, bouncing on the spot.

Otis stares at him, annoyed that he interrupted, and baffled as to why he is incapable of finding his own way to the toilets. He appears to have an incessant need for attention.

The landlady continues to wipe some glasses, and scrutinizes Jefferson for a few moments. *He is an acquired taste,* Otis thinks.

'And you are?', the landlady asks.

'Jefferson Riley', he replies, puffing his chest out proudly.

'Famous influencer', he adds.

Otis cannot help but be amused; it is like Jefferson is a caricature of himself.

'Jefferson Riley, eh? Never heard of you', the landlady says, placing the glass down harshly on the worktop.

'Come with me then', she barks at him.

Jefferson about turns, and follows her like a schoolboy would a teacher. The group is left waiting in the deserted pub.

'Think it may be colder in here than it is outside', Kiki says, sounding disappointed.

The landlady returns a few moments later; casually walking past the new arrivals as if they are not even there. She flings a tea towel over her shoulder, and continues to stack some glasses.

'Didn't even think trains still stopped at that station; think they're closing it down soon', she says without looking up.

'Er... like I said, I don't suppose you have a working phone or WI-FI. Seeing as none of our mobiles have signal', Otis presses.

The lady shrugs her shoulders and begins wiping down the bar with the cloth.

'Yeah, you won't find any network here, it's always been a total dead zone for miles. Wi-Fi though? Yeah, we do have that', she replies.

The group look collectively relieved.

'Ain't working though. Assume the storm has knocked it out', she continues.

Otis sighs. He spots a landline phone behind her, and gestures towards it hopefully. The lady titters, shaking her head.

'Ah yes, isn't it great how all phones are digital now instead of analogue. Really handy in situations like this', she says.

The group sighs again. Otis has had enough of standing around.

'In that case, I'll take a whiskey please', he says.

He heads over to the bar and hops onto one of the stools. The landlady throws a cardboard coaster in front of him, along with a scratched looking glass. Blowing some dust off the bottle cap, she pours him a big glug. Otis takes a sip; it tastes cheap and nasty. He may have an inkling why this pub is empty.

'Miranda', she says.

'Oh, Otis', he replies.

'Nice to meet you', she says.

The group remain by the doorway. Otis glances back at them.

'Well, what else are you going to do?', he says, raising his glass before taking another sip.

The group look around at one another before choosing to join him.

'Red wine please', Daphne says, perching next to Otis. They exchange a smile.

'Almond de-caff flat white', Jefferson says, having returned from his bathroom break.

The landlady raises an eyebrow. The group look on, feeling amused and already unsurprised by his demand despite their short time together.

'Black coffee or no coffee', she replies flatly.

'This is going in my vlog', Jefferson mutters under his breath.

Kiki shakes his head in bewilderment, unsure exactly what kind of vlog that would be.

'I'll take one of those black coffees, ta', Kiki says.

Muhsen decides not to join the others near the bar, choosing instead to sit in one of the booths at the front, by a window. He still clutches his phone.

'I'm sure the Wi-Fi will come back on soon', Otis calls out.

Muhsen manages a grunt of acknowledgement but fails to tear his eyes away from his device. Otis finds him a peculiar young man, full of anger and frustration.

Jefferson sits down at one of the nearby tables and begins fumbling his hair with his hands. It takes Otis a minute to realise he is trying to style it; the unruly waves fail to yield to its master. Otis is a little perplexed why Jefferson thinks his hair style is the most important thing right now. That question is soon answered, as Jefferson holds his phone in front of his face.

'Hi everyone, I am recording this from an adorable little country pub off the beaten track. My journey home took an unexpected turn, but sometimes the unexpected leads to life's best adventures. As I always say, just enjoy every turn in the road as you never know where it will take you. I don't know when I'll get to upload this, but when I do I know you'll enjoy the show I have for you. Catch you all soon, and remember kindness is King', Jefferson says with a wide grin.

Otis tuts, then quickly slaps his hand over his mouth realising he sounded like Jefferson. Daphne laughs.

'He's rubbing off on you', she says.

'Never', Otis says.

'I won't judge you if you want to vlog about how amazing you think this experience is', she continues.

'You should judge. Kindness is King? He was like a different person as soon as the camera was rolling', Otis says, with a wry smile before sipping some more whiskey.

'Urgh, what a dive', Jefferson mutters.

Daphne leans towards Otis.

'Guessing the vlog is over', she whispers.

Otis chuckles silently. He looks around the pub; Jefferson is not wrong; it is a dive. Dusty and unloved. He even questions how it could possibly still be in business if this is a typical night.

Miranda watches Jefferson: Otis is unable to tell if she is amused or displeased by the resident vlogger.

'It's quiet tonight', Otis observes.

'Always is these days unfortunately. Not much passing trade', Miranda says.

She looks a little downcast after that remark; Otis chooses not to pry further.

'So, what's your story', Miranda says, shifting her attention.

She pours Daphne a generous glass of wine.

'M-me?', Daphne says, taken aback.

Daphne looks around at the others wondering why she was chosen.

'Yeah, don't worry I'll work my way round everyone', Miranda says, with an air of mischief.

'N-no story. Just on my way to an appointment', Daphne says.

'Always the ones that say they have no story, that end up having a really good story', Miranda says.

Daphne pulls out her book from her bag, wishing to immerse herself in a fictional tale. She takes a sip of her wine and grimaces; it tastes acidic. She tries to hide her disgust from the watchful eye of the landlady.

'Oh, you're into crime thrillers, are you?', Miranda asks, reading the cover of her book.

'Bit of a guilty pleasure, yes', Daphne says.

'Ever thought of starring in one?', Miranda asks.

Daphne inadvertently snorts, as a sudden laugh comes out through her nose instead of her wine-filled mouth. She pinches her nostrils, which now burn from alcohol.

'Bit of a random comment. You mean like be an actor? No, I don't think so. I'm quite happy just reading them', Daphne says, shooting an amused look at Otis.

Jefferson scurries around the pub, trying to take artistic shots of the interior.

'I'll have to photoshop most of this', he mumbles irritably.

Kiki makes some smart remark to Jefferson, causing him to put his phone away and storm off towards a table on the other side of the room. Otis could not make out what words were exchanged, but one thing is certain: they are polar opposites destined to always clash.

'Nice ring', Miranda says, noting the yellow-gold ring with a knotted heart on Daphne's wedding finger.

'I had something similar once from one of those claw machines at an arcade', Miranda continues.

Daphne shuffles in her seat, and hides her hand as if ashamed.

'Oh, hey I'm sorry. I didn't mean to imply it was cheap or nothing', Miranda says apologetically.

'No, it's fine', Daphne replies.

Otis feels the apology was lacking in substance. Miranda heads out the back to fetch the coffee. Otis watches Daphne open her book, but notices her eyes do not move.

'It's a nice ring' Otis says sympathetically.

Daphne half smiles.

'I'm not really married anymore. He... he died', she says.

'Oh, I'm sorry', Otis says.

He takes another sip of whiskey. The detective in him wants to know more, but it seems crass to pry for the sake of prying.

'It is pretty cheap', Daphne says, studying the ring on her finger. 'But that's never the point, is it?'

Otis nods, finding himself increasingly intrigued by this stranger.

'I tell you what else is cheap', Otis says, pointing at their drinks.

Daphne raises her wine to that; they chink glasses.

The sound of crashing glass makes both him and Daphne jump; for a moment they think they have broken their own glasses. They jerk around to see what the cause of the commotion was, to find Kiki and Jefferson in a stand-off. Jefferson has knocked some of the stacked glasses off the side.

'You pillock! You take that back!', a red-faced Jefferson shouts, pointing a finger at an amused looking Kiki.

'What on earth happened?', asks Otis.

'This dope thinks I'm a con artist', Jefferson says.

Kiki smiles and shakes his head.

'I merely said being an influencer is two-for-a-penny these days. Nothing special', Kiki says.

Otis spots Jefferson's fists clenching.

Otis stands up, getting ready to break up a fight, but hoping to defuse the situation before it reaches fever pitch. Daphne gets ready by downing her drink quickly; she goes cross-eyed momentarily from the bitterness of the wine, slightly regretting her decision.

'Jefferson, I'm sure Kiki didn't mean your job wasn't important. Just that it's very popular. Lots of people would like to be a successful influencer', Otis says pragmatically.

Kiki smirks.

"Yeah, that's what I meant', he says.

Otis shoots him a look, one that a teacher may reserve for a wayward student.

'Hey!', Miranda cries, appearing from the back with a dustpan and brush. 'If you lot are going to trash the place then you can clear out now'.

Everyone retreats to their seats in silence. Only the sound of broken glass being scraped into the dustpan can be heard.

'What are you lot planning to do anyway? This pub closes in 30 minutes', Miranda says, looking at the lost travellers.

They all stare back at her looking non-plussed.

'You can't throw us out there', Muhsen cries.

He looks outside as the rain starts to fall. It hammers on the window like a shower of nails. As he stares into the darkness, he thinks he spots something moving but cannot be certain. He edges closer to the window and squints, trying to make out anything beyond the splashes of water on the pane, and his own pitiful reflection.

'What's up? Do you see something?', Miranda asks.

Muhsen jumps, unaware that the landlady had moved so close to him. She leans over and peers out the window.

'You'd have to be a fool to be out there in that', she says. 'I can't see anything.'

Muhsen fidgets awkwardly, not comfortable with his personal space being abruptly invaded by a stranger. Miranda gives a quick wipe of the table in front of Muhsen, before sitting on the seat opposite him.

'I'm sure I saw something moving out there', Muhsen says.

'Of course you did, it's blowing a gale', Kiki calls out.

'You sure you don't want a drink?', Miranda asks Muhsen.

'Yeah, I'm sure', he replies.

Miranda watches Muhsen twitch under her stare. He taps at his phone once again.

'Is someone expecting you?', Miranda asks.

'What? Yeah. I'm part of this tech start-up event', he replies.

Miranda nods thoughtfully. She looks around the pub.

'So, do any of you lot know each other?', she asks.

Muhsen shakes his head.

'Jefferson likes to think everyone knows him, fancies himself a celebrity', Muhsen says with more than a note of disdain.

Miranda glances back at Jefferson.

'Yeah, he is a bit of a funny one', she says quietly.

She leans back against the worn seat cushion, and observes Muhsen for several seconds. His fingernails appear recently chewed, and his shoulders remain permanently hunched; he seems unable to avert his attention from his phone for longer than a minute. *Tightly wound,* she thinks.

'Quite the entrepreneur then?', Miranda persists.

Muhsen makes some sort of sound; Miranda cannot be sure if it was even a word. *Quite the chatterbox too,* Miranda jokes to herself.

'Right', she says extra loud, to grab people's attention.

Everyone in the room turns to look at her. Muhsen drops his phone, much to his horror.

'Seeing as it looks like you are all staying here until the morning comes, I suggest you set up camp in the back living room. Get to know each other', she says with an impish grin.

Daphne leans into Otis.

'You don't think she means in a kinky way, do you?', she whispers.

Otis almost spits out his drink; he begins to cough and splutter.

'Can't say that crossed my mind! But I hope not', he says trying not to choke on the stray whiskey droplets trapped in his throat.

'Can't you drop us into the nearest large town?', Jefferson asks, looking appalled by the thought of staying here the night.

Miranda looks at him, with a slight hint of scorn.

'Firstly, why should I? Secondly, I don't drive. I don't have a car', she says.

Jefferson looks aghast.

'No car? You're in the middle of nowhere', he says.

Miranda looks irritated.

'My husband drives, and he's returning home tomorrow morning. I'm sure he'll oblige you with a lift. Or…' she says, looking towards the door, 'you're welcome to walk the few miles up the road in this storm. Perhaps someone in the tiny village of Dillingford will open their door to you in the middle of the night, and agree to drive you wherever you want in this weather.'

Various looks are exchanged between the strangers; everyone feels aggrieved by their limited choices. Miranda smiles smugly; she brushes past Otis and Daphne who are still perched at the bar, and grabs two bottles of spirits and some glasses. Miranda turns to look at her guests, and raises the bottles in the air, gesturing for everyone to follow her. Otis detects that she is enjoying playing the hostess to, what probably has been, the largest crowd in here for a while. She has the look of someone who has suffered more than one knock in life; a hardened exterior, but Otis wondered whether a softer interior lay within.

The living room is cold; there only seems to be one source of heat in the room, a fire which is currently unlit. Jefferson makes a beeline for the armchair; he proudly sits in it as if it were a throne. Kiki and Muhsen sit on the sofa; Kiki gestures for Daphne to take the final available seat. Daphne looks back at Otis.

'It's alright you take it', he says, reaching for a wooden chair tucked under a desk in the corner.

The other armchair has been left for their gracious host, who is currently lighting the fire. Only the rain and Miranda's several attempts to strike a match can be heard. With the fire finally lit, Miranda heads back out of the room.

The strangers sit staring at the flames as they slowly come to life. No one is able to relax, their bodies are rigid from the chill. The whole pub has a slight damp, musty smell to it. Of all the quaint country pubs there are, Otis feels cheated to have ended up in such an un-cosy one.

BANG.

A huge boom reverberates through the walls, and everyone is plunged into darkness. The light of the fire is still too small to fully penetrate the dark. Gasps and shrieks ensue.

'I swear there is something on my leg!', Daphne screams.

'Calm down everyone', Otis says. 'Can someone find their phone light?'

A bright light partially fills the room; it comes from the sofa and swishes from side to side. More lights join. Otis checks on Daphne, who looks bashfully at him, having realised it was the strap of her bag that she had felt on her leg.

'Like I said earlier, imagination runs wild in the dark', Kiki says to her.

Miranda re-enters the room, delicately clutching a lit candle.

'Struck by lightning. You're a jumpy lot, aren't you?', Miranda says calmly.

'It's been a funny sort of evening I think it's safe to say', Kiki says.

'I'll keep checking the phone line. Your loved ones must be worried', Miranda says.

Everyone nods except for Kiki.

'No?', Miranda asks, spotting Kiki's lack of head movement.

Kiki turns a little red.

"Well, not all of us are blessed with love', he says solemnly.

The room falls silent. No one knows how to respond.

'Gosh what a gloomy sod you are!', Jefferson says.

'Jefferson', Otis says, shaking his head and gesturing with his eyes towards a glum looking Kiki.

'Oh, come on! There's bound to be someone somewhere who will miss that round little face of yours', Jefferson says to Kiki.

'No. We can't all be as well-loved as you, Jefferson', he replies flatly.

Kiki avoids everyone's gaze, choosing instead to focus his entire attention on his shoes. Daphne wonders what kind of events must have happened to Kiki for him to make such a damning statement at a young age. *Nursing a fresh heartbreak perhaps,* she thinks. She is eager to learn more.

'Okay let's call time on this conversation', Otis says.

Daphne looks deflated by this proposal; a good love story would have been a great distraction. She scans the room, desperately trying to find inspiration for an alternative topic. It is no good, she decides to stubbornly persist with the original subject.

'It's good to talk about things sometimes', she says to Kiki quietly, 'I'm told I'm an excellent listener.'

Kiki continues to stare at his shoes.

'I lost my husband', Daphne says, hoping to open the door to conversation. Kiki remains silent. Daphne finally concedes this topic is a non-starter.

'They're dead', Kiki whispers.

Daphne looks startled. She looks around to see if anyone else heard, but no one appears to.

'Who?', she asks.

'Family. But I don't want to talk about it', Kiki says.

Unfortunately, all this has done is make Daphne even more intrigued. She clasps her hands together in frustration, her mind full of questions.

Miranda leaves the room again. Otis can hear the faint sound of drawers and cupboards being opened and shut in the distance. She returns clutching some candles, and distributes them among the group, along with matches. Everyone silently begins lighting and placing them wherever they can around the seating area. The place begins to feel a little cosier.

'Very atmospheric', Miranda says, taking a seat.

'Who's that?', Daphne asks, her eyes fix on a framed picture of a couple embracing. The man has a huge grin and proudly stands in the doorway of the pub, with his arms wrapped around a woman who looks equally proud. The outside of the pub looked a little more spruced up back when the photo was taken. Miranda turns and stares at the picture silently for a moment.

'Oh, my sister and brother-in-law. They had the pub originally before passing it on to me. They are in Australia now', Miranda says, keeping her eyes on the picture.

Otis looks around the room, there are no other photos or ornaments.

'I like the minimalistic look', Miranda says, catching Otis's eye.

'How long have they been in Australia?', Daphne asks, trying to get some conversation flowing in the group.

'Oh, several years now', Miranda says.

Daphne is disappointed by the lack of detail and storytelling. She sighs, contemplating what a long, dull night this is going to be. Everyone takes a long sip of their drink; a cheap whiskey that burns the throat. The only nice thing about it is the fact it takes the edge off the cold. Muhsen declines having any. Although still slightly on edge, the alcohol does appear to be having a calming effect on the rest of the group.

'We've got a fire, candlelight, whiskey, and a storm raging outside. Think it's the perfect evening to share some stories', Miranda says.

Everyone immediately feels less relaxed.

'What kind of stories?', Kiki asks.

'Hmm, one story about yourself that we'd all find interesting, or surprising', Miranda suggests.

Everyone looks at each other, shuffling awkwardly in their seat.

'Reserved lot aren't you?', Miranda says.

'Why don't we start with something a little more generic. Like why this pub is named The King's Feet?', Kiki asks.

Miranda takes a swig of her drink.

'Ah, now that I can tell you. Folklore spins a tale of a King; a man not merely measured by the many wives he acquired, but of the feet he measured. You may describe yourself today as, for example, six feet, but you are actually six of our King's royal trotter.'

'Huh. Well, I wasn't expecting that', Kiki says.

'I was. I knew it would be dull', Muhsen says.

Otis once again finds himself defusing a salty atmosphere.

'Thanks, Miranda', he says.

She gives a harsh side eye in the direction of Muhsen.

'Perhaps we should move on to sharing some stories from our own lives', Miranda says.

'Go ahead', Kiki urges.

Miranda slowly sips her drink, and stares thoughtfully at the ceiling.

'I saved a sheep once', Miranda replies.

Everyone looks at her; whatever story they were expecting, they had not anticipated it would be this. She continues:

'It was stranded and sinking in a mud pit. I almost killed myself in the process. I battled for well over an hour to release that poor little mite. Do you know what the worst thing was? Other people had walked by and left it because it was too difficult. Fancy leaving something to die, because saving it was difficult.'

Otis wonders why that story was picked out of all stories; it seemed to lack substance, which made him even wonder if it were entirely true.

'Well, I applaud you. I can't bear to see any animal suffer', Daphne says, raising her glass to Miranda.

As Daphne takes another swig of the awful whiskey, she feels endeared to see that there is a softness to the landlady that had remained hidden until now.

'I would have just left it. I mean, why bother? It is only a sheep', Muhsen says.

Daphne looks mortified.

'You could watch something die?', she says, feeling vexed.

Muhsen barely manages a shrug; he appears unbothered by her reaction.

'Death is part of life', Muhsen replies.

This time it is Miranda who chooses to step in and defuse things. It is proving challenging to make this group of strangers get along.

'Think you volunteered to be next', Miranda says to Daphne.

Daphne takes an even bigger sip of whiskey, as she stalls for time.

'I really can't think of any story', Daphne says.

No one responds. Everyone waits patiently.

'Well, this is peer pressure at its finest', Daphne jests. 'Fine okay, well I guess if I had to pick one story about myself it would be how I met my husband. On the beach of Torquay, I sat reading a terribly cheesy love story; thinking to myself how unrealistic it was. You know, the classic: woman is happy alone, until a man literally saves her from some sort of ridiculous situation. Well anyway, I suddenly heard what I thought was the shriek of a woman. I jumped up and ran over to the rocks to try and work out if she needed help. Except, instead of a woman I found a rather handsome and muscular man. He had slipped and got his foot trapped between two rocks. He was trying to watch a crab of all things', Daphne says, smiling from ear to ear. 'It was in that moment, I knew this shrieking, crab-loving man was the one for me.'

'Ah, the classic love story came true – except he was the damsel in distress', Otis says.

'And you lived happily ever after I guess', Jefferson says with a yawn.

Otis glares at him. Daphne tucks some stray strands of hair behind her ears, her smile disappears.

'No. Not exactly. He died', she says.

Jefferson takes a big glug of whiskey, unsure what to say.

Kiki gives Daphne a few gentle taps on the shoulder.

'Well, I'll go next', Kiki says, hoping to break the sudden sad atmosphere. 'I'm named after a parrot.'

This rivals the sheep story, Otis thinks.

'Yep, my mother's first child was an African Grey she called Kiki, whom she got when she thought she couldn't have kids. She was devastated when he died. So, when I surprisingly came along, Kiki the 2nd was born. Apparently, we were similar: talked too much, overdramatic, needed constant attention.'

Kiki laughs softly. Otis and Daphne share in his amusement.

'So, you *do* have someone who loves you, your mum', Jefferson says cockily.

Kiki stops his gentle laughter abruptly, retuning his gaze towards his feet.

'She died', Kiki says.

Jefferson rolls his eyes.

'God, this is a cheery night', Jefferson says.

Daphne feels sorry for Kiki; clearly, he is grappling with a lot of grief and pain. She tries to suppress her curiosity about what he had said earlier.

'Right, come on then Jefferson. Dazzle us with one of your stories', Otis says, feeling increasingly irked by his constant eye rolls.

'I have a thousand stories you can all enjoy when you subscribe to my Vlog', Jefferson says, stroking his phone as if is some sort of prized treasure.

'Why don't you tell us a genuine story, one that is not made for show', Kiki says.

Jefferson's face turns sour; he clearly disliked this comment. He slams down his glass, almost missing the table. Everyone feels on tenterhooks, unsure if they are going to get a story, or an argument.

'Alright then. You want a story? How about I wish I was dead. There! The end', Jefferson says, slurring slightly.

'I think maybe ease up on the whiskey', Otis says.

Jefferson sticks his middle finger up at him.

'Charming', Daphne says.

'Why do you wish you were dead?', Miranda asks, looking a little alarmed.

'Because when everyone thinks you have everything, it often means you have nothing of worth', he says drunkenly.

He looks at Kiki like he is vying for a fight; Kiki looks away, unsure how to react and not keen to engage with an increasingly intoxicated Jefferson.

Miranda does not seem to know whether she should look worried or amused.

'I think that's the end of story time', Otis declares.

'Good', Muhsen hisses.

'Oh, you got out of it', Miranda replies.

Muhsen grumpily looks back at his phone. He is the least engaged of everyone. Kiki puts down his glass and turns towards him, looking perturbed by Muhsen's persistent sulking.

'You could at least be a little more civil, you know? You're not the only one who had their plans ruined', Kiki says.

'What right have you to tell me what to do or how to be?', he retorts.

Muhsen does not even bother to look up from his phone.

Kiki seems further riled by the lack of eye contact; Daphne notices his fingers digging into his lap, as if trying to hold himself back.

'Everyone has the right to point out when someone is being a miserable, rude, idiot', Kiki says.

The whole atmosphere in the room changes. Everyone stares down at the floor, unsure where else to direct their attention.

'I think we're all tired. It's been a stressful evening', Otis says, hoping to bring some civility back to the night.

'He's the one with the problem', Muhsen argues.

Everyone knew he directed that comment at Kiki, despite still refusing to take his eyes off his phone. Before Kiki can fire out his next response, he is interrupted by a sound.

Knock-knock-knock.

The unexpected knock of the door brings any further conversation to a halt. Miranda glances up at the clock, it is 12am.

'Wonder who that could be at this time', she says, getting up from the chair and heading out of the door.

Otis notes she looks a little apprehensive. She returns moments later looking confused.

'No one was there', she says.

'How strange. Perhaps it was the wind?', Daphne suggests.

Chapter 3
A Stranger's Passing

"When death comes knocking, bolt the door."

Once again, an uncomfortable silence falls. The mutual feeling of wanting to be anywhere but here is palpable. Otis glances over at the three other men, who all look miserable and barely make eye contact with one another. Jefferson pours some more whiskey for himself. The storm is reaching its peak outside; the windows rattle from the wind, which howls as it whips around the walls of the pub like a sinister ghost.

Knock-knock-knock.

Everyone looks at each other. Miranda straightens up in her seat. She glances at the clock again: 12.06am.

'Um… Muhsen would you come with me this time?', Miranda asks.

Muhsen looks a little shocked at being asked. He opens his mouth to speak, but no words come out. Otis is also surprised she asked him, of all people, to go. Muhsen shuffles silently out through the door with Miranda.

'Never heard a wind knock like that', Otis says to Daphne.

'No. Perhaps it's not the wind. The rain?', she says optimistically.

Otis looks sceptical.

'Bit of a stretch, maybe', Daphne concedes. 'It's just I don't know if I like any other options beyond the weather.'

Otis strains to listen to the distant sound of Miranda and Muhsen's voices; he cannot detect a third voice although it is hard to hear clearly over the storm that rages outside. The sound of hurried footsteps in the hallway draws closer. Miranda and Muhsen return, each wearing a puzzled expression on their face.

'No one was there', Muhsen says suspiciously.

He sits back down and begins to rub his shin, pouting like a child.

'You alright?' Otis asks.

'Knocked my leg on a stupid chair. So dark out there!', he snaps.

'It's kids I bet. You see it all the time. Tricks played on people, filmed and put out on social media to generate an audience. Of course, I don't partake in such low brow content', Jefferson says, picking lint from his sweater.

Muhsen and Kiki both shoot Jefferson an exasperated look.

'Bit late for kids', Miranda says.

'And we're in the middle of bloody nowhere', Muhsen interjects.

'I can't work it out. Who on earth would be out in this, and for what purpose', Miranda says, clutching a nearby cushion for comfort.

Jefferson looks ill at ease, he takes another big swig of alcohol. Wiping his mouth with the back of his hand to remove some residual whiskey, he gets up and goes to one of the windows. He presses his face against the pane and hovers there for a while.

'Do you see anything?', Miranda asks.

Jefferson moves unsteadily back to his seat.

'I think I would have told you by now if I had', he replies.

Miranda looks unimpressed by his tone.

'If it knocks again, I think I'll go', Otis says to Daphne, in hushed tones.

'Does seem rather peculiar', Daphne says.

'What about this night isn't?', Otis replies.

Muhsen maintains his pout; he reminds Otis of how a young child looks when they are unable to get their own way.

'There must be a way to leave this stupid place, I have things to do', Muhsen says.

Otis can tell Kiki is increasingly irked by Muhsen's rudeness to the host. In fact, all three of the other men appear to have taken an instant dislike to each other.

'Feel free to head out there on your own', Miranda says, looking offended.

'You may all think I'm being rude, but I might end up missing a business deal bigger than any of you could imagine. A deal that would finally mean I'm free', Muhsen says passionately, underpinned with resentment.

'Free from what?', Daphne asks, ever intrigued by other people's tales.

Muhsen leans back on the sofa and folds his arms, reluctant to give away anything further.

'Just the family business', Muhsen mumbles.

Daphne stares at him, waiting for him to tell her what that is. He appears more susceptible to her than the others.

'Butchers', he replies finally, succumbing to her eager stare.

Being a vegan, Daphne is unsure what else to do with this conversation.

The group settle down once more, starting to appreciate the warmth of the log fire. Kiki pulls out a notebook and begins scribbling ideas for poems. Jefferson sinks further into a drunken stupor. Muhsen shoves some headphones in his ears. Daphne studies her temporary companions, and their lack of social interaction.

'I think we're the only ones who like each other', Daphne says to Otis.

Unsure how to reply, Otis quickly takes a large sip of his drink. *Nice to know she thinks I'm likeable'*, he thinks.

'So, where were you heading before this eventful detour?', Daphne asks.

Otis tries to think quickly; the truth is not something he is willing to share.

'Just to attend to some unfinished business in Hammersley. You?', Otis says nonchalantly.

'For reference, when someone says they have unfinished business then it often means they are hiding something', Daphne says peering over her glasses at him.

She smiles. Otis feels like he is on the backfoot; he adjusts his collar. Daphne decides to shift the conversation, for his sake.

'I actually have a job interview in Hammersley first thing in the morning', Daphne says.

She raises her hands in the air and gives an exaggerated shrug.

'I'm guessing I won't make it now', she says.

'You never know', Otis says.

'Thing is, not sure if I really wanted it. I'm a bit of a free spirit when it comes to jobs. Hate the nine 'til five desk job that you keep for years and years. I like a bit of variety. I like to help people. Solve problems. I often wondered about joining the Police, but I'd only break all the rules', she says.

Otis laughs. He had an increasing desire to get to know Daphne further.

'What is the job for?', Otis asks.

'Oh, it sounds so dull. It's working for Southern Train Company's communications department. Truth be told, I only got an interview because my best friend works there and is trying to get me into more stable employment', Daphne says.

'So, what unstable employment are you currently in?', Otis asks.

Before Daphne can reply, a familiar sound interrupts them.

Knock-knock-knock.

Everyone moves to the edge of their seat, their senses now on high alert. Miranda glances up at the clock: 12.12am.

'Good lord! Who on earth is playing silly buggers at this time of night, and in this weather!?', Kiki cries.

'I'll go', Otis says, standing up and urging everyone else to remain where they are.

He disappears confidently through the doorway. Daphne hurries to the window but it faces out towards the side of the pub, making it hard to see the entire front area. In the light it would be possible to see some of the road and driveway, but the rain continues to slam into the glass, making it near impossible to see outside.

Otis walks cautiously towards the door; he looks around the candlelit pub which has an eerie feel to it. Even the hairs on Otis's neck begin to stand to attention. He tries to peer through the side window next to the door, but can see nothing except his own faint reflection. Reaching for the key, he turns it slowly and takes a step back as he opens the heavy wooden structure.

Otis is greeted by nothing but splashes of rain, as the wind sends flurries of droplets through the doorway. He slowly steps over the threshold and holds up the light on his phone, moving it from left to right. All he can see are the flashes of water shooting towards the ground. There appears to be nothing around the entrance that could be causing the knocking sound. Otis reaches for the door knocker in the shape of the wolf's head, and gives it a gentle knock. It is heavy and stiff, and unlikely to be easily swayed in the wind.

Closing and locking the door, he turns back towards the bar and brushes some of the rainwater from his clothes.

Something catches his eye on the floor; it is a pink lip balm. He bends down and picks it up, and places it on the side of the bar before heading back down the hallway.

Otis returns to the living room with the same perplexed expression as the previous door openers.

'Let me guess, no one there', Jefferson says with his signature eye roll.

Otis nods. He turns towards Miranda.

'You had any trouble like this before?', he asks.

'No. Never', she says. 'It makes me feel quite nervous.'

'Don't worry', Otis says peering through the crack in the curtain and craning his head to look down towards the deserted street.

'Daylight will be here in a few hours, and we can try and get to the bottom of it then, if it keeps happening', he says.

Miranda continues to hug a cushion tightly.

'To be honest, I do feel better not being alone tonight. Fortuitous you lot arrived. Probably we best get some shut eye. It'll be a bit of a squeeze I'm afraid', she says.

Daphne scans the cramped room, hoping to shut herself away somewhere private for the night.

Unable to sit around any longer, Miranda stands up and begins dishing out orders to her edgy house guests, keen to get everyone settled.

'Muhsen, there is a cupboard in the landing upstairs with some more blankets and pillows. Grab some and distribute them around the two bedrooms along the same corridor. Bring some back into this room also. Otis, go out into the back courtyard and get some extra logs from the shed – the fire will go out during the night otherwise. Kiki, can you check the doors and windows are all secure in the pub, and draw the curtains. Daphne, take all these empty glasses through to the kitchen just a bit further down the hallway', she says.

'I can tell you're used to being in charge', Muhsen says.

Miranda ignores this comment, detecting a touch of sass.

'Fortunately, there's a gas hob so you can make some hot drinks too', Miranda tells Daphne.

Jefferson hiccups loudly, as he sinks deeper into the cushions.

'Ah, Jefferson, nearly forgot you!', Miranda says.

'Perhaps I'll stay here, finish this', he says holding up a bottle of whiskey and tipping out the last remaining drop.

Miranda frowns.

'Hmm, perhaps that is best, looking at the state of you', she says quietly. 'I need to sort some crates in the cellar ready for a delivery tomorrow', she says to the rest of the group.

Jefferson sits back in the chair with a satisfied grin on his face, as he watches everyone disappear to carry out their assigned tasks.

The property is old and has thick walls and doors; little can be heard of the guests as they carry out their duties except for the occasional bump. The noisy weather further shields any sounds. Otis can barely hear himself think under the tin roof of the log shed; he feels he drew the short straw with his particular task. He loads as many logs as the basket will carry, before making a mad dash back across the small rear courtyard. The rain attacks him without mercy; he has no time to take in any more of his surroundings.

Re-entering the house, he rushes down the corridor and past the open door of the kitchen, without glancing inside. The basket is heavy, and he can feel it slipping through his wet hands. His clothes are soggy, his body shudders as the damp seeps through to his skin; he is eager to dry them quickly by the fire. As he turns into the living room, he sees Miranda at the end of the hallway facing away from him, her hands full of small packets of nuts and scratchings.

'Oh, Kiki? Sorry my hands are full. Can you check the door? I'm sure I heard another knock!', she calls out into the bar area. 'I'm starting to think it really is the wind', she adds.

As Otis re-enters the living room, he finds a wobbly Jefferson staggering back to his chair.

'Where have you been?', Otis enquires.

He receives no response; Jefferson barely acknowledges him. Otis places the basket next to the dwindling fire. He turns to head back out to assist Kiki but suddenly a bottle flies towards him, hitting his stomach. He grabs it before it drops to the floor. He looks towards Jefferson, startled.

'S-sorry...', Jefferson slurs. 'But I... need a re-re-refill'.

Otis assesses the sorry state that greets his eyes. *An influencer under the influence,* he muses to himself. Jefferson's eyes are as read as his cheeks, and his recently combed hair is now a jumbled mess.

'I think you've had more than enough', Otis replies sternly.

Otis places the bottle down and begins to walk towards the door but is interrupted from leaving once again, this time by the sound of a sudden thud from the corner of the room. He turns around to discover Jefferson has slid off the chair; Jefferson looks around in complete astonishment as to how he came to be there. Otis takes a deep breath in, before striding over to encourage him back up onto the seat.

'I wasn't always like this you know', Jefferson mumbles, 'Sometimes you're driven to do things.'

Otis feels an unexpected tinge of pity for Jefferson. *Perhaps his online alter ego has become too dominant,* Otis thinks. Jefferson almost slides off the chair again. Otis shakes his head and stands next to him for a moment to ensure he remains seated.

'People tear you down. But never as much as you tear yourself down', Jefferson drunkenly rambles.

Otis stares down at him, pondering what he just said. He chooses to stay with him. Rapid flashes of lightening illuminate the room momentarily, highlighting Jefferson's face and further exaggerating the look of drunken madness that fills his eyes.

'Gosh he's in a bit of a state, isn't he?', Miranda says.

Otis twists his neck around abruptly, and discovers Miranda placing the snacks on the table behind him.

'I didn't even hear you come in', he says.

'I could see you were dealing with something', she says, looking at Jefferson.

'Yes, the drink seems to have taken possession of him', Otis says.

Muhsen returns to the living room, looking as glum as ever. He heads for the window and stares out into the darkness; what he hopes to see in the pitch-black night, Otis did not know.

'Wasn't pleasant being out in that I can tell you', Otis says to Muhsen, trying to make conversation but to little avail.

Having successfully managed to stop Jefferson sliding off the chair twice, Otis commences battling the fire.

'Well, someone doesn't mind being out there', Muhsen says.

Miranda quickly rushes to the other window.

'Why, do you see someone?', she asks.

'No. But someone obviously is. Doors don't just knock like that on their own', he replies.

Everyone pauses and looks at each other with worried expressions.

'Well, we don't know for sure–'

'Oh, quit with trying to be reassuring. No one is reassured. Nothing about this situation is reassuring', Muhsen says, cutting across Otis.

Otis chooses not to reply directly, and instead shifts his attention back to tending the fire. Miranda hovers over Otis, watching his hard work.

'I'll go and assist Kiki now', Otis says, placing the last log on the fire.

Daphne enters the room with a tray of freshly poured tea.

'Who was at the-'.

Miranda pauses, as she turns and sees Daphne entering.

'Oh, sorry I thought it was Kiki returning', she says.

'Nope, just little old me I'm afraid', Daphne replies, placing the tray carefully on the coffee table.

Daphne heads back to the doorway and peeps her head out.

'Kiki, come get a cup of tea whilst it's still hot', she calls, unsure of his exact location.

She pauses and listens but hears no response. Everyone sits around the coffee table and reaches for a cup. Otis nudges the semi-conscious Jefferson.

'Come on, grab a cuppa, it'll help sober you up', he says.

Jefferson grunts and turns the other way. Otis exchanges a coy smile with Daphne.

'Lightweight', Otis says, looking at Jefferson.

Daphne looks towards the doorway.

'Wonder what's keeping Kiki', she says.

'I'll go check on him', Otis says.

'He's not a kid, he'll be fine', Muhsen snaps, much to everyone's surprise.

Otis looks over at Muhsen, who avoids his gaze.

'Still, I think I'll just see what's keeping him', Otis says firmly.

Otis takes a few deep slurps of tea; his throat feels dry from the fire.

'Wait up', Daphne says. 'I'll come too.'

'Prft. So suddenly he needs a whole search party', Muhsen says.

Daphne and Otis look at each other, both confused by his apparent misdirected anger. They choose to ignore him, and proceed to walk out of the living room. Muhsen watches them leave, stewing in his own irritation.

Miranda stretches her arms high in the air and yawns, eager to have a rest from this tense atmosphere.

'Right, I don't know about you two but I'm off to bed. I'll let you fight over who sleeps where', she says, with a wave of her hand towards Muhsen and Jefferson.

'There's the sofa and chairs down here, and then just up the stairs there are the two spare bedrooms opposite each other. No idea what state they are in as their hardly used, so I'll apologise now for any dust', Miranda continues.

A piercing scream reverberates down the hallway, so loud that it even causes Jefferson to stir from his drunken drowsiness. Everyone in the living room freezes momentarily.

'Daphne?', Miranda calls.

'Quick come here!', Daphne shouts.

'Where are you?', Muhsen calls.

'The bar. The bar!', Daphne screams.

Miranda leaps up and heads out of the door, followed by a hesitant Muhsen. Jefferson looks around the now empty room, perplexed by everyone's sudden departure.

'Hey, where are you all going', Jefferson says rubbing his eyes. 'What's happening? W-wait for me.'

He scrambles to his feet and unsteadily makes his way out of the room, following the sound of animated voices.

Everyone is stood in a semi-circle, staring at something on the ground near the front door. Jefferson edges closer, knocking into a barstool causing everyone to jump; he pushes his way through to see what they are looking at.

'Good god!', Jefferson yells.

The lifeless body of Kiki lies face-up on the floor. Blood seeps from his neck and encircles his head. His eyes stare blankly at the ceiling, robbed of any previous sparkle.

Chapter 4
Alone Together

"To feel alone surrounded by people, is the heaviest isolation to bare."

'Has someone checked if he's breathing?', Jefferson cries, averting his eyes from the unmoving body on the floor.

Otis bends down and feels for a pulse. Everything is still. Not a single pump of blood can be felt. He studies the source of the blood loss.

'His throat has been slit', Otis says. 'He would have bled out almost instantly.'

'Who would do such a thing!? And in my pub!', Miranda says.

Daphne swallows, deeply suppressing the urge to be sick. She turns away from the body and looks around the pub.

'No sign of a struggle', she observes.

There are no overturned chairs. No signs of anything being out of place. Otis follows Daphne's gaze. Their eyes come to rest on the door.

'It's unlocked', they say in sync.

Miranda marches to the window next to the door and looks out.

'I can't see anyone, although it's very dark', she says.

'Oh, come on! Whoever did this will be long gone by now! Not going to hang around, are they?', Jefferson says.

'What do we do?', Daphne's voice trembles.

'We need to stay calm and work out how to get help', Otis says.

'We need to get out of here', Muhsen shouts, pacing the floor.

The shock of Kiki's murder has done little to sober Jefferson. He leans against the bar for support. Scoffing disapprovingly, he mutters how everyone is being stupid.

'Wouldn't want you lot around in a crisis', Jefferson says.

'Shut up Jefferson! Why are you so calm when there is a psycho somewhere who just murdered Kiki', Muhsen shouts.

'He's drunk, he doesn't know what he's saying. Or doing for that matter', Daphne says to Muhsen, trying to calm him down.

'I think you lot need to stay calm like me, and look at all the facts', Jefferson says, slurring his words slightly.

Otis already found a sober Jefferson irritating, but a drunken one is much worse.

'Well,' Otis says, stepping backwards and gesturing towards Kiki's body with his arms, 'Go head.'

'What?', says Jefferson, looking both puzzled and tipsy.

'Run the show. Solve the murder. Tell us what to do next', Otis replies, allowing his annoyance at Jefferson to get the better of him.

Jefferson eyes Otis up and down with suspicion, and a tinge of annoyance.

'I don't need to solve anything. All I know is I should walk out that door right now and leave this pub', Jefferson says.

'Interesting', says Otis. 'You're obviously confident there is no murderer lurking outside, or else you wouldn't want to go out there.'

Jefferson seems stuck for words.

'Well, no. I mean, yes. I mean, I don't know where the murderer is! It could be one of us', says Jefferson, his eyes dart around the room suddenly spooked by the fact everyone is now staring at him.

'Perhaps, as the Landlady of this pub, I should take charge', Miranda says.

'The way I see it is we have a dead body and murderer somewhere on the loose. Naturally, we are going to feel on edge about those immediately around us, even though it seems likely the murderer knocked the door, stabbed Kiki and departed', Miranda says.

Otis tries to interrupt but Miranda presses on.

'Before you say anything, I am merely basing that on the evidence of the door knocks, and the fact the door was unlocked. I'm happy to be proven wrong.'

She hesitates.

'Well, not happy as that would mean one of us—anyway, all I am saying is we should simply go around the room and state our alibi to put everyone at ease.'

Miranda looks over at Otis who gestures for her to go first, being the proprietor of this plan and of the pub.

'I was in the cellar preparing the crates for the morning delivery. The cellar is pretty much soundproof so I'm afraid I didn't hear anything. As I came up from the cellar with some snacks for us, I thought I heard a door knock and asked Kiki to check. I then went back into the living room where Otis and Jefferson were', Miranda says.

'So, not an alibi then', Jefferson says.

'Well, actually I did see you call out to Kiki. I then went into the living room', Otis says.

'See, I have a witness. I was with Otis in the room, after he had seen me in the hall', Miranda says.

I have no idea exactly when you entered the living room, Otis thinks. He estimates perhaps five minutes had passed between seeing Miranda in the hallway, and noticing she was in the room with him and Jefferson.

'So, what was Kiki doing when you saw him last?', Otis asks Miranda.

A look of realisation flashes across her face.

'Oh, I actually didn't see him. I just thought I heard him round the other side of the bar towards the fireplace area. Last I knew, he was drawing all the curtains for me. He didn't respond, now I come to think of it. Although, I went straight to the living room so maybe I didn't hear him reply?', Miranda says, as she tries to piece together the puzzle.

Everyone's eyes dart around the room. *Did Miranda hear the murderer?*, Otis thinks.

'And you didn't have a view of the front door between leaving the cellar and the hallway?', Otis asks.

He walks over to the hallway entrance; the view of Kiki's body is blocked by a large pillar and some tables.

'The cellar?', Otis asks, looking around for its location.

Miranda walks behind the bar and around the corner. Otis follows her, and then takes the route from the cellar entrance back towards the hall. He glimpses Kiki's shoes sticking out but that's about it.

'It's not a clear view', he says to the rest of the group, who watch him with anticipation. 'The flickering candlelight does little to help.'

'What about you then, Jefferson?', Miranda asks.

'Well, I... um I don't remember much. I was in the living room and never left my seat', Jefferson says.

'So not an alibi then', Miranda says sarcastically.

Jefferson's cheeks turn red.

'I did see you walking back to your seat from somewhere, when I returned with the logs', Otis says.

Jefferson stares back at him; he looks like a deer in headlights.

'I didn't go anywhere', Jefferson protests.

'Perhaps you're too drunk to remember', Miranda says.

Everyone uneasily stares at Jefferson for a few moments, trying to determine if beneath his superficial demeanour lay murderous intent. Miranda then shifts her gaze to Muhsen.

'Me? Well, I went upstairs to fetch blankets, and I went into the spare rooms. I didn't hear or see anything', Muhsen says.

'I see', Miranda says, raising an eyebrow.

Muhsen is fidgety, unsure what to do with his hands without his phone grasped within them.

'Why so nervous?', Miranda asks.

'I'm not nervous! What are you implying?', Muhsen says angrily. 'Why would I kill Kiki? I didn't even like him.'

Otis has never heard such a flawed justification for not killing someone. Jefferson leers at Muhsen whilst reaching for a bottle of brandy on the side of the bar.

'I don't wish to sound like a stickler, but I think it's best to keep your head clear for when the police arrive', Otis advises Jefferson.

Jefferson inhales dramatically and places his hand on his chest, as if he has been accused of something terrible.

'That goes for everyone', Otis says looking around.

Jefferson reluctantly places the bottle back down on the side.

'Well, Otis, you seem quite the leader of the pack. Let's come to you next', Miranda says.

Otis leans back against the bar, arms folded in front of him.

'Do I?', he replies. 'Well, I've been called worse things.'

'So long as one of those things isn't a murderer', Muhsen says under his breath.

Muhsen seems surprised that he let this comment slip out of his mouth. Otis does not hear; he meets the gaze of Miranda.

'Why are you so confident?', Miranda says, unblinking in her determination not to break eye contact first.

'I was a Police Detective for a long time', Otis says.

The atmosphere of the room noticeably shifts; a mix of relief and nervousness collides.

'Why didn't you mention this sooner?', Muhsen says.

'A retired Police Detective now', Otis says with a hint of sadness.

Daphne detects some resentment in that statement, a look of anguish flashes across his face.

'Anyway, I went out the back to retrieve some logs. On my way back to the living room I heard you, Miranda, call to Kiki to go to the door and check if someone was there. I was going to go myself but someone', Otis gives a stern look towards Jefferson, 'needed attending to.'

Jefferson fails to show any kind of humility. Daphne clears her throat; she appreciates an encouraging glance from Otis.

'I was in the kitchen washing up and then making the tea. I didn't see anyone, or hear anything', Daphne says.

Daphne self-consciously strokes her hair, looking disappointed in her own story that provides little clues to the crime. Being an avid lover of reading mysteries, she found herself surprisingly caught off guard being thrust into the heart of a real one. A feeling of sorrow and excitement bubbles inside of her.

Miranda walks behind the bar and picks up the phone.

'Still out', she says, before disappearing down the hall for a moment.

Muhsen peers out of one of the windows once again; it is becoming a nervous twitch for him.

'Can't see any life out there, assume power is still out everywhere', he says.

Otis reaches into his back pocket and pulls out his phone. There is still no network. He mulls over what to do.

'Yep, everything is definitely still out', Miranda says, returning to the bar.

Daphne lets out a faint whimper, her eyes widen as her head fills with more thoughts.

'What if someone is hiding inside the pub?', she whispers.

Everyone looks at her, frozen to the spot.

'That is a valid point' Muhsen says. His twitching returns with a vengeance.

Everyone remains where they are, not wishing to be the first to move.

'Okay fine let's split into groups and check the different areas of the pub', Miranda says eventually.

'Split up? I don't know about that. What about safety in numbers?', Daphne says, turning to Otis.

Otis considers this for a moment, both options had their merit.

'I think if we split into two groups, it lessens the chance of someone being able to elude us. We can cover more ground in parallel', Otis says.

Otis spots Daphne's unconvinced look.

'I think it unlikely anyone is hiding', he says trying to sound reassuring.

'Nevertheless, be vigilant', he adds.

'And what exactly are we to do if we are confronted with a homicidal maniac?' Jefferson demands.

'Scream and hope the other group comes to your rescue', Miranda says dryly.

No one moves. No one is keen to go looking.

'Come on, we can't stand around here. Let's put our minds at rest that no one is hiding anywhere', Otis says. His heart starts to beat a little harder.

'Okay, who's coming with me then?', Miranda asks.

'I'll come and assist you, in exchange for some more free booze', Jefferson says, still eyeing the bottle of brandy he had been forbidden to open.

'Jefferson!', Daphne yells, wishing they had never had any alcohol at all.

'It's fine, I've encountered worse during my time as a landlady', Miranda says.

'We'll check the upstairs, you check the downstairs', she continues.

Miranda grabs a half-empty bottle of whiskey as they leave.

'Our weapon', she says to Jefferson.

'Will you be okay with him?', Otis asks, not convinced if anyone should be left alone with him.

'Of course. Besides, if I turn up murdered then you'll know exactly who it is', she says crassly.

She's a peculiar tough cookie, Otis thinks.

Otis, Daphne and Muhsen are left standing in the sudden eerie quiet of the bar area. Both Daphne and Muhsen appear to be waiting for Otis to give them a command.

'What are you thinking?', Daphne asks Otis, noticing he is deep in thought.

'The weapon? There is no sign of it. It appears to be a small, sharp blade. Could even be a peeling knife. One, sharp swipe of the carotid artery and Kiki would have gone into shock and bled out', Otis says.

Daphne continues to suppress the urge to be sick. Otis notices her pale complexion.

'Basically, whoever did this knew what they were doing?', Daphne replies.

Otis nods solemnly.

'Well they either took the knife with them, or hid it somewhere', Daphne says looking around the area where Kiki lies.

'Surely, they would take it with them. Why leave incriminating evidence to be found', Muhsen interjects.

The wind lets out an almighty howl, causing the old windows to rattle. Otis feels a chill run through him. Daphne looks terrified. Muhsen maintains his angry, suspicious stare.

'Okay, let's walk around in the direction of the toilets first, near the fireplace', Otis says.

They stay close together, almost too close. Otis feels like he has two children clinging to him. The candlelight plays tricks on them, making the shadows move and dance around them.

'I took some karate and self-defence classes once, but now it comes to possibly using them in the real world, I can't remember anything', Daphne says.

'A petite thing like you? You're best just running', Muhsen says.

Daphne feels partly offended and partly complimented.

'I'm much stronger than I look. I lift weights you know', Daphne retorts.

'Alright you two', Otis says, hoping to instil some silence.

They turn the corner, where there is a small enclave. Within it are two doors, each to a separate toilet.

'You go and I'll keep watch', Muhsen says to Otis.

'Gee thanks', Otis replies.

Daphne looks unsure what to do. She chooses to follow Otis but remains tucked in behind him, as if he is her shield. Otis silently counts to three and reaches for the handle of the first toilet. He throws the door open quickly, readying himself. It is empty. They all exhale in relief, before turning towards the second toilet door. The hold their breaths again. Otis takes a little longer to open the door this time, he listens for any sound coming from within. *1,2,3*. He flings open the door. Nothing but an empty cubicle greets them.

'Not sure my heart can take much more', Daphne says clutching her chest.

'Well, this bar area is empty but what about the cellar?', Daphne asks as they head back towards the scene of the crime. They look past the bar, down the hallway that leads to the living room on the left, the stairs on the right, and then the kitchen at the back.

'If you're going to hide anywhere, it'd be a dark cellar', Muhsen says.

They walk around the back of the bar, following its L-shape towards the cellar door which is shut.

'Good luck', Muhsen says turning towards Otis.

Otis raises his eyebrows. *The cheek,* he thinks.

'Have you lot even moved?', Miranda says, appearing from the hall with Jefferson lagging behind her.

'No sign of anyone in the upstairs rooms, kitchen or living room. We checked them all as we passed', she says.

'I think they've guessed that, based on the fact they didn't hear us scream and run for our lives', Jefferson mocks.

Miranda shoots him a disapproving look.

'Otis was just about to check the cellar', Muhsen says, edging away.

'Oh. Well, the cellar should be locked. I always lock it overnight. It would be a burglar's paradise to get hold of the stock down there', Miranda says.

'So, you locked it before you came back into the living room?', Otis asks.

Miranda nods and walks to the entrance of the hallway, where a box with a keypad is drilled to the wall. She keys in some numbers and pulls the door of the box open, pointing to a hook with a large iron key dangling from it. Otis heads to the cellar door and slowly turns the handle. It is still locked. Before Otis is able to speak, he is interrupted by the sound of tapping. This time, it appears to be coming from the direction of the back door at the end of the hallway. Everyone holds their breath; their eyes fill with horror.

'Otis, maybe you should go?', Muhsen says.

Absolute bloody cheek, Otis thinks. He frowns at Muhsen.

'Perhaps we should all go this time', Otis says.

Tap-tap-tap. Tap-tap-tap.

They all head nervously down the darkened hallway. Otis holds his redundant phone in front of him; its sole purpose now is to light his way. He sees his battery flash a warning: less than 10% power left. They pass the empty living room on their left, and then the kitchen to their right. Straight ahead of them is the brown back door, with a small window set within it. Otis cannot see anything but the darkness beyond the glass pane.

Tap-tap-tap.

'We need a weapon', Jefferson cries.
'A knife from the kitchen?', Muhsen suggests.
Otis halts and turns to look at the nervous faces behind him.
'I don't think we want to bring anymore knives into this. Besides, we shouldn't touch anything that may be linked to the crime scene', Otis says.
He spots a walking stick propped up in an umbrella stand. He pulls it out and holds it out in front of him.
'IF there is someone there, we just need to restrain them. Let's not become homicidal maniacs ourselves', he says.

Tap-tap-tap.

Daphne squeezes the back of Otis's arm.
'Be careful', she whispers softly.
'Right, I'll open the door on the count of three. Remember, if there is someone there and they appear to want to harm us then we restrain them. I'll aim for a weapon

if there is one. Jefferson, Muhsen you get ready', Otis says, trying to sound calm.

Jefferson and Muhsen look alarmed at being singled out. Muhsen adopts an even angrier face in preparation. Jefferson moves his clenched fists around in front of him like some sort of dance.

What could possibly go wrong, Otis thinks.

'1,2,3.'

Otis reaches for the handle; the door is unlocked. He flings it open and shines his phone light out into the darkness. There is no sign of anyone. Muhsen and Jefferson slowly edge closer, bringing the lights from their phones into black of the night. Everyone remains quiet. Otis looks around the sides of the doorway. He spots a semi-broken branch swinging nearby in the wind. He directs the others to step back inside, as he closes the door from the outside. He watches the branch swing towards the top of the door.

Tap.

Opening the door again, he is greeted by an array of startled eyes looking intently at him.

'Hmm. Think that may have been the source of the tapping', Otis says pointing up at the dangling branch from a nearby tree, that sits at the edge of the courtyard. Otis manages to tuck the branch behind a protruding bit of wall with a trellis on, in the hope that no more tapping will occur. He then closes the door and makes sure to bolt it. Otis briefly presses his face against the door window and looks out; it's impossible to see anything through the drips of water.

'Let's go back into the living room', Otis says.

No one argues. Everyone funnels slowly towards the warm glow of the fire. Re-entering the room, Daphne gives a sad glance at the now vacated seat where Kiki had sat a mere hour ago; he had been so full of spirit that it is hard for her to comprehend the brutal fragility of life.

Chapter 5
Trust All but No One

"Deceitful souls pray on the faithful."

'Dillingford is a few miles away. We have two options. We wait here together for a few hours, and as soon as sunrise comes, we go out and see if someone can drive us into the nearest town; or the power may have returned by then. Option two, some of us try to walk to Dillingford now, and see if someone can get help', Otis says.

'The latter', Daphne says immediately.

'It's at least a three mile walk in the pitch black, and in a storm. Do we even have torches, as my phone battery is ready to die', Muhsen says gloomily.

Right on cue, a loud crack of thunder rings out above them, followed by several lightning flashes.

'And we still don't know for sure that no one is out there', Muhsen continues.

'Or... maybe the former option then', Daphne says quietly.

The rain seems to have got increasingly heavy. Daphne is not sure what is worse; being outside in the middle of nowhere in that, or being in here with a dead body. *It would help if I knew if the murderer was inside or outside*, she thinks.

'Let's stay in groups at least, whatever we choose to do', Miranda suggests.

'Fat lot of good that is if you're paired with the murderer', Jefferson says. 'Nope I don't need a chaperone, thank you.'

Miranda shrugs.

'Okay', Miranda says. 'Makes you seem pretty guilty though.'

Otis detects an imminent argument.

'Jefferson, leave it. Don't pick another fight', Otis says.

'I agree with Miranda; it makes sense to always have someone else with you whenever possible', Otis says.

'All I have is candles, no torches', Miranda says.

'My phone probably won't last the walk either', Jefferson adds.

Seemingly left with little option, a feeling of dread washes over the group, as they realise they must wait out the storm together.

Otis remains standing, whilst the rest of the group return to their previous seats. He takes out a tin of mints from his jacket pocket and pops one in his mouth. It helps him think. Everyone is watching him expectantly.

'So, we have searched the house and there is no sign of anyone. We have each stated our alibis. Now, let's turn our attention to the weapon. A small-bladed knife. Possibly a kitchen knife. Firstly, in the same spirit of sharing our alibis, let's all demonstrate that we have no such weapon in our possession', Otis says.

He picks up his satchel and proceeds to take out the items inside: a notebook, pen, pack of tissues, and a small toiletry bag with a few essentials in. He shows the now emptied bag to the room. No one knows how to respond.

'Right, who else has a bag?', Otis says, as he repacks his satchel.

Daphne pulls her backpack onto her lap.

'I just have this', she says, beginning to empty its contents.

She blushes as she reaches in for the final item.

'Um… well I was just staying overnight so I have…'

She pulls out a pair of knickers.

Otis turns red.

'Okay, that's enough. Thank you, Daphne', Otis says quickly.

She quickly stuffs the black laced garment back into her bag, slightly relieved she at least packed one of her more decent pairs.

'I don't have a bag. All I need is my phone', Jefferson says, waving his device in the air to emphasise his point.

'Weren't you wearing a backpack?', Daphne asks.

Jefferson shakes his head.

'Nope. You're thinking of Muhsen', he replies.

Muhsen has a sleek looking computer backpack. Otis is not surprised by its contents: tablet, laptop, cables. All currently useless to him. Muhsen begrudgingly empties it and shows everyone.

All eyes now fall on Miranda. She laughs a little.

'Well, this whole house is my bag', she says.

Everyone appears to have the same thought, as they each begin looking around the room for signs of a possible hiding place for a knife. The room was fairly sparse. The only obvious place would be the drawer in a desk in the corner. Miranda spots Otis's curious look towards it.

'Be my guest', she says.

He walks over and opens the drawer. It contains nothing but a single pen rolling around in the back.

'That desk is purely decorative now', Miranda says.

Otis closes the drawer, and proceeds to slowly walk around the room, studying it for any signs of a useful knife nook. Aside from the chairs, sofa and coffee table there is not much else to the room in terms of furnishings. It feels practical rather than comfortable, and perhaps last decorated in the 80s.

'Okay, I think I've seen all there is to see in here. Miranda, would you mind coming to the kitchen with me?', Otis asks.

'The kitchen?', Miranda says, looking confused.

'Yes. I want to check whether any of your knives are missing. Everyone else, stay together in here', Otis says, casting a serious look around the room.

As Otis and Miranda leave, Daphne takes another look around the room.

'Hang on, where did Kiki's bag go?', Daphne asks, looking around the area where Kiki last sat.

Muhsen shrugs, and Jefferson appears surprisingly disinterested.

'Well that's very strange', Daphne says, peering under the sofa.

Upon Otis and Miranda's return, they confirm that nothing appears to be missing. Miranda returns to her armchair. She sighs heavily.

'In fairness, if someone did knock the door and attack Kiki then that knife will be long gone from here', Miranda says.

Otis contemplates what to focus on next; should he continue to search for a weapon that may be miles from here by now, or should he re-examine the crime scene?

'I wonder if someone would mind coming with me into the pub area? There is something I want to check', Otis says.

Daphne gets up straightaway.

'I'll come', she says eagerly.

'Um... excuse me but who made you the lead detective?', Jefferson says with a hiccup, the alcohol still filling his veins.

'My commissioner did back in 2010', Otis says matter of factly.

Jefferson stares with wide eyes.

'We covered this earlier, Jefferson', Muhsen says shortly. 'You need to sober up!'

'Don't worry, I may be retired but detective work... well it's like riding a bike', he says, flashing a smile around the room.

He observes the array of expressions that greet him. A face flushes red, a nervous smile, a scowl, an eye roll.

Otis and Daphne exit the living room, leaving their fellow suspects in uncomfortable silence.

'I assume you really were a detective and that wasn't some story to set the cat among the pigeons?', Daphne says as they walk down the corridor.

'No, it was all true I'm afraid', Otis says.

'Why afraid?', she replies.

He shakes his head.

'Oh, nothing', he says dismissively.

'So, what did you want to check?', Daphne says looking around the room.

'I just wanted to try and piece together his last moments', Otis says. 'We know the reason he was in the pub area was to check the doors and windows. So, let's assume, given he is by the door, he was in the process of checking it. Either someone came through the door unexpectedly, or he opened the door to someone.'

Otis rubs his chin and studies the way in which Kiki's body is lying with his head nearest the door.

'Or did someone approach from behind?', Otis ponders, still rubbing his chin but with a little more vigour now.

Lost in their thoughts, Otis and Daphne are taken by surprise by the arrival of the others.

'She wanted to come and see what you were doing', Jefferson says, pointing towards Miranda.

'Well, it is my pub', Miranda says.

Otis feels a migraine coming on. He continues with his musings.

'Given there is nothing for miles around, it seems unlikely a random person knocked the door with the intent to murder', Otis says.

'Unless someone was following Kiki?', Daphne suggests.

'We'd have seen if someone was, surely', Otis replies.

'Although, those door knocks were strange. It's like they kept knocking until the right person came to the door. Was the right person Kiki?', Miranda says.

'I admit those knocks were odd, and puzzling', Otis says.

'And what hasn't happened since Kiki was killed? A door knock', Daphne replies.

Muhsen huffs impatiently.

'I think it's pretty obvious. Someone was outside, they knocked the door, and for whatever reason when it was Kiki's turn to open it they killed him. Who knows what he may have been caught up in; we didn't know him. I think the bigger question is, why are we not locking that door?', Muhsen says crossly.

Everyone looks at the unlocked door. Miranda leans over and reaches to turn the key.

'No', Otis says, raising his hand to stop her.

'We really shouldn't touch anything, even the key in the door. Anyway, if anyone tries to come through, they'd have to get past him', Otis says, looking down at Kiki's body which now acts as a doorstop.

'Should we at least cover him up?', Daphne says, feeling increasingly nauseous.

Otis can see her turning a pale shade of green.

'Okay, a light bed sheet ought to be fine', Otis says.

Miranda nods and hurries down the hall. Everyone stands quietly, unable to look at Kiki. Otis studies each one of them; they all look as queasy and uneasy as each other. Miranda rushes back through the door holding a white sheet. Otis takes it, and very gently lays it on top of Kiki. He is overcome by a surge of poignancy as he finds himself at the scene of another unnecessary violent death.

Everyone re-enters the living room feeling helpless but clinging to a hope that they will soon be free from here. Daphne is eager to continue discussing possible suspects and scenarios with Otis, but is hesitant to discuss too much in the presence of everyone else. She watches Muhsen who is stood in the corner, curtain twitching again, his face filled with anger. Otis has also spotted the increasingly enraged look on his face.

'Why don't you sit down?', Otis says.

'Piss off', Muhsen says sharply.

'You rude little-'

Otis interrupts Daphne with a gentle nudge. She glances at him; he gestures for her to say nothing.

'Not worth it', he says to her quietly.

'Can't see anything!', Muhsen says furiously, flicking the curtain closed.

He runs his hands back and forth through his hair, as if overcome with nits.

'He seems almost at breaking point', Daphne whispers into Otis's ear.

For a split-second Otis is overcome with a strong feeling of fondness for Daphne, as her warm breath hits his skin. He feels guilty over the inappropriate timing of such a thought. Daphne stares at him through furrowed brows.

'Are you okay?', she asks, spotting his suddenly pink cheeks.

'Yes, breaking point. Him… I mean', he says clumsily, nodding towards Muhsen.

Otis feels as if Daphne is reading him like an open book; her emerald eyes stare intently back at him.

Miranda watches her guests curiously, pondering what she should do with them all. She observes the outwardly confident Jefferson, seemingly eager to get on everyone's bad side. She studies Muhsen, who carries the biggest chip on his shoulder that she has ever seen. Finally, her eyes settle on Otis and Daphne, mere strangers yesterday but thick as thieves today.

'Look, I suggest we all get some rest. Hopefully the internet will be back up and running soon, and as soon as light comes it'll be easier to head to the village, or with any luck my husband will be back', Miranda says.

She glances up at the clock, the time is now 2am. No one feels compelled to go to sleep with a dead body in the house, and a murderer *somewhere*.

'I find it ridiculous we are all just going to go to sleep, with a murdered body in the other room', Jefferson cries.

'And what kind of messed-up place is this with no internet or phone network. How can we be in the soddin' 21st century and unable to reach anyone?', Muhsen rages.

The group appear to be unravelling. Otis is no longer an official detective, but he feels compelled to try and steady the ship, and bring some order.

'Listen, I was a detective for several years. I've investigated many murders. The odds of a murderer sticking around in this situation are slim', Otis lies.

'We just need to keep it together until the storm passes and the sun rises, then we will get help here', Daphne adds, in a bid to assist Otis in his quest for calm.

Otis looks at Daphne appreciatively. Jefferson looks around the room with his hands on his hips, on the brink of stamping his feet.

'I'm going to say it even if no one else will. I don't feel safe sleeping in the same room as any of you. Personally, I would prefer to barricade myself in a separate room', Jefferson says.

'Yeah, can't say I'm compelled to shut myself in a room with you lot all night', Miranda agrees.

Otis sighs. Times like these he missed his official Police badge.

'I tell you what, Daphne and Muhsen you take one of the spare rooms each. Jefferson, you take the sofa. And-'

Otis interjects Miranda's plan.

'And I will take one of these chairs and stay in the hallway', he says.

'I'll be fine', Otis dismisses Daphne's concern before she is able to say anything.

'Why are you sleeping in the middle of the hall?', Miranda asks, looking stunned.

'I don't intend to sleep; I plan to keep watch. Reassure everyone', Otis says.

Miranda is surprised by his plan.

'You want to plonk yourself out in the dark hallway all night, completely exposed?', Jefferson says to Otis, whilst grabbing a wooden chair from the corner.

'Where are you going with that?', Miranda asks.

'I'm not sleeping unless something is jammed up against the door', he says, dragging the chair across the room with rhythmic thuds.

'Fine', Miranda says with her arms in the air.

Jefferson ushers everyone out of the room, and promptly shuts the door. Everyone hears the thud of the chair being shoved against the handle.

Miranda gestures for Muhsen to head upstairs.

'Spare room on the right', she says.

Muhsen looks apprehensive.

'Muhsen, you can take a chair too. No one would blame you for being scared. Anyway, I'm heading up', Miranda says.

Muhsen stands on the spot for a moment before deciding against the chair. He straightens his posture in a show of strength and courage. However, Otis has no doubt that Muhsen is as afraid as everyone else. Otis listens for the two doors to close upstairs before going to grab a chair to put in the hall. Daphne loiters in the hallway for him.

'You best get some rest', he tells her.

Daphne turns to head upstairs but changes her mind. She spins to face Otis again.

'I', she lowers her head looking deep in thought.

'What is it?', Otis asks.

'I don't know why, but I trust you. So, there'll be no chair against my door', she says.

Otis smiles awkwardly. Unsure what to say next, he encourages her to get some sleep.

'Although, having a chair would protect me from the actual murderer I guess', Daphne says, looking baffled at her previous comment. 'It was meant to be a nice compliment, but I think it was a flawed statement.'

Otis chuckles.

'I think you need to give your brain a rest from thinking too much', he says.

'It's hard not to. I keep flicking between the culprit being within these walls to being beyond them. Have you got any theories about all this?', Daphne asks.

Otis puts the chair back down, and leans against it as he rattles through his thoughts.

'If we purely look at opportunity, then any of us could be the culprit. Indeed, anyone outside could have done it. If we look at motive, well, that's where it gets tricky. None of us knew Kiki so I am struggling to find one', Otis says.

'Unless someone really hates people named after parrots', Daphne says.

Otis looks a little startled.

'Sorry, bad moment for a joke. Go on', Daphne says, her face suddenly feels very warm.

Otis laughs a little.

'Well, yes. So, then let's look at means. Kiki appeared to be killed by a small knife. So where is it?', he says.

Daphne frowns.

'It could be anywhere. Thrown into bushes outside. Miles from here with the murderer. Who knows?', Daphne says.

'Hmm. Quite', Otis says, deep in contemplation.

'Perhaps a more prudent question is, where did it come from?', Otis says quietly.

'If we take at face value that no knife is missing from the kitchen, then it suggests the murderer brought it with them. And the only people who travelled with bags are us and Muhsen', Otis continues.

'So, you seem to be looking for a suspect within these walls rather than outside? I thought you said the chance of the murderer sticking around was slim?', Daphne says.

Otis gives her a warm look of reassurance but offers no words to accompany it, leaving Daphne to wonder what he is truly thinking.

'I can't lie, the thought of someone within these walls being capable of murder makes me feel very scared about sleeping here', she says.

'I'm not surprised! But that is why I'm positioning myself at the base of the stairs, where I intend to remain awake all night', Otis says.

'That's good to know. Unless you're the murderer of course', Daphne says, with a nervous chuckle.

Otis does not respond. He positions his chair and takes his seat.

'Night', he says.

Daphne wonders whether he actually heard what she had said.

'Okay, well… night then', she says.

Daphne heads up the stairs clutching one of the many candles that had been lit; the whole place feels eerie. She feels sure she is being watched by someone other than Otis. Before entering the bedroom on the left, she glances at the two other bedroom doors, both of which are shut. The wind and rain make it hard to hear if there is any movement. She peers back down the stairs and is pleased to see Otis keeping a watchful eye. Otis tries not to enjoy watching the silhouette of her figure from the base of the stairwell; whatever feeling he is beginning to have for Daphne, it is not one he has had before. A sense of ease radiates through him whenever he is alone with her, as if she has always been part of his life. As Daphne enters her room for the night, the landing gradually turns very dark as her candlelight disappears from view, leaving Otis staring up a stairway to nothingness.

Despite her best effort the candle will not light every dark corner of the bedroom, no matter where she positions it. She unplugs one of the lamps, after double checking the power is definitely still out. Crawling on top of the lumpy, old bed she clutches the lamp tightly, a makeshift weapon. *Just in case.*

'Well, this is fun', she says to herself.

At least Otis is keeping guard, she thinks. If it were not for this, Daphne is not sure that she would be able to stomach being in this room alone.

Leaning back in the uncomfortable chair, Otis is determined to remain awake. Not a single sound can be heard, except for the continued trickle of the rain outside. All is quiet in the living room; it would not surprise him if Jefferson were continuing his drinking spree. Looking up the stairs, he has an albeit dark view of the square shaped landing between Muhsen and Daphne's room. Just beyond that, is Miranda's doorway. The minutes tick by in silence; Otis feels his eyes getting heavy, and his body exhausted from the brutally long day. His mind, overloaded with thoughts, gradually begins to empty with every tap of the rain, gently sending him to sleep with its soft lullaby.

Chapter 6
Scattered Seeds

"Which comes first, motive or means?"

'You let him get away!'
The child appears, tugging at Otis's arm once again.
'I tried. I tried!', Otis cries.
'Otis? OTIS? You're dreaming', Daphne calls out.

Otis awakes to Daphne's concerned face peering over him. Her elegantly tied-back hair is now loose and dangling a mere inch from his face; he can smell the faint apple scent of her shampoo. His eyes struggle to open fully, as they adjust to the early morning light starting to stream in through the window.

'Oh, I... ouch!', Otis mutters, as his back cracks and clicks as he tries to pull himself up from his awkward position on the wooden chair.

Every bone in his back aches. Beyond Daphne, Jefferson and Miranda are stood and look equally perplexed. Otis quickly wipes some dribble from his chin, feeling increasingly self-conscious

'What the hell was that all about?', Jefferson says.

'Nothing', Otis replies, wishing a hole would gobble him up.

Daphne rests her hand gently on his arm.

'Are you sure you're okay?', she says softly.

Somehow, Otis is not irritated by Daphne's concern. In fact, he seems to enjoy it, much to his astonishment.

'Yes, just a strange dream', he says. 'What time is it?'
'5.30am', Daphne replies.

'Well, isn't this marvelous, a dead body and a psycho ex-detective. You couldn't make this up', Jefferson says, pushing his way past Daphne who remains stood by Otis's side.

Daphne spins around to face Jefferson.

'Oi, you little shit, now listen here – you may think you are some big hot shot celebrity, but that doesn't mean you are. In fact, none of us have heard of you. And frankly, right now, the way you carry on makes you suspect numero uno in my mind. So, you better keep out of my way or else I may choose to join social media and post one or two stories of my own', Daphne says.

Jefferson's mouth is wide open as he backs away from Daphne. Otis and Miranda look equally taken aback. Otis cannot help but smile a little though; it was no bad thing to bring down Jefferson a peg or two. Daphne looks flustered, embarrassed by her sudden outburst.

'Sorry. He just irritates me', Daphne says.

Unclenching her fists and flicking her wrists, she tries to release the built-up annoyance that has been festering. Jefferson scurries down the hallway.

'Always the bloody quiet ones you gotta watch', Jefferson says in hushed tones.

Daphne helps Otis up; more bones click into place.

'Gosh, I miss my youth', he says.

'Don't we all', Miranda says, appearing behind them and following Jefferson out towards the bar.

'Suspect numero uno?', Otis says to Daphne, with a raised eyebrow.

'Oh, well. I don't know. I guess finding someone arrogant doesn't make them a murderer' she says.

'Not always', he replies.

Otis walks gingerly down the hallway towards the bar. Miranda has begun opening the curtains; the world outside teeters on the edge of sunrise. The shifting light and break in weather brings a sense of hope and relief to the weary strangers.

'I'll be there now, just need to find my glasses', Daphne tells Otis.

As Miranda and Otis enter the bar area they find an increasingly agitated Jefferson staring at the draped body on the floor.

'I just need air. I can't breathe in here', Jefferson says, rushing past them and back out of the bar.

Otis glances over at Kiki. He recoils at the brutal sight of it. The once pure white sheet is now almost completely red, and clings to his body; Otis can see the outline of every button on his tweed jacket. Miranda picks up the phone.

'Still no connection', she says.

'What?', Otis cries.

'I know, I prayed it would all be back working this morning', Miranda says forlornly.

The sound of the backdoor banging shut makes both him and Miranda jump.

'Let's get some air, take a look outside', she suggests.

Otis stretches his arms behind him, appreciating the few more clicks that ripple through his back. He follows Miranda down the hall, passing the living room where Daphne has commenced her glasses search.

'Come get some fresh air, see things in the light of day', Otis calls to her.

Daphne pauses her search for her glasses and follows him outside. The air is damp and chilly. Remnants of the strong winds remain. Opposite the back courtyard is a garage, surrounded by trees. Otis joins the others at the top of the driveway near the lane; the area is so peaceful. Only the morning birdsong can be heard, as the sun slowly wakes the world. There is nothing but undulating fields as far as the eye can see.

'Is the garage locked?', Otis asks, eyeing it with curiosity.

'Yes, always is. Only thing we keep in there is my husband's car. He's quite precious about it', Miranda replies.

She looks at the garage then looks back at Otis, studying his quizzical face.

'I doubt anyone would be hiding in there all night. Not only would they struggle to get in but what would be the point?', Miranda says.

'When is your husband due?', Otis asks.

'Not for another two hours or so, I imagine', Miranda says.

'I'll have to walk to the next village. We can't keep hanging around like this. It's not as if this is on a busy road with ample people passing by', Otis says, feeling frustrated.

'It's a wonder you're still in business', Otis says shortly.

He notices Miranda visibly recoil at this remark, making Otis regret his curtness.

Daphne looks into the distance; she rubs her eyes that itch with tiredness.

'You alright?', Otis asks her.

'I need to find my ruddy glasses', she replies.

Otis turns and heads towards the porch area of the pub front door, leaving the others to enjoy the freedom from the pub walls. He surveys the area, looking for any signs that someone may have been there last night. Daphne soon joins him.

'What are you looking for?', she asks.

'Not sure really. You always know when you see it', Otis says.

Daphne scrunches up her face again, and helps him look.

'What's that?', she says, pointing to an object on the ground right in front of the doorway.

Otis squats down to take a closer look.

'It appears to be an empty chewing gum wrapper. Could have been there long before last night of course. Hard to know', Otis replies.

They both head back towards Miranda and Jefferson, concluding there is nothing more to be found.

'Otis, at least have a drink of water before you go', Daphne insists.

She eyes him with concern; he looks pale and pained. Feeling disappointed at the lack of civilisation outside, all except Jefferson head back inside.

'I just need a few more minutes in the fresh air. I'm not feeling good this morning', he advises the group, clutching his stomach.

'Hardly surprising, given what you put away last night', Daphne says.

Unusually, Jefferson does not have a smart retort.

Otis heads to the kitchen with Miranda whilst Daphne resumes her search for her glasses.

'How are you feeling this morning?', Otis asks Miranda, sipping some water.

She looks tired; like everyone else, she remains in the same clothes she wore last night.

'Awful. I'm not really sure how much I slept. I tried to fight closing my eyes for as long as I could', she replies.

Otis feels ashamed of his failed attempt to remain awake, although relieved that nothing else happened during the night. If it had, his shame would soon turn to guilt. He is not sure how much more guilt he is able to carry on his shoulders.

'Otis, come quick!', Daphne cries out from the direction of the living room.

Otis and Miranda look at each other with dread, before rushing towards Daphne. As they enter the room, they find her standing near the door pointing in the direction of the armchair where Jefferson had been sat the previous night.

'What is it?', Otis says.

Otis rushes over and leans across the chair; something red is sticking out between the cushion and the arm.

'It looks like some sort of sheath', Otis says.

'That's what I thought', Daphne says.

'You didn't touch anything?', he asks.

'No. No, of course not. I just spotted it when I was looking around for my glasses', she replies.

'What are you both talking about?', Miranda asks.

Otis gestures for Miranda to come and see.

'It looks like it's for a knife', Otis says, looking around the room for something to use to pick it up. He grabs his satchel and pulls out a handful of clean tissues. Gently lifting the sheath up, he realises it is empty.

'Yeah, definitely looks like this contained a small knife', Otis says carefully studying it.

Just at that moment Jefferson enters the room.

'What are you doing?', he demands.

'What are you doing, more like', Miranda retorts.

She points towards the sheath.

'Care to explain it', she says.

Jefferson stares at the object nestled within the tissues, as Otis places it down on the table.

'It's a holder for a knife, found hidden down the side of the armchair where you were sat most of the evening, in a room where you slept all night', Miranda says to Jefferson.

His face is pale. The group of strangers stare inquisitively at him wondering if he is sick from guilt, or sick from alcohol.

'Well, I... I mean, I don't know how that got there. I've never seen it before in my life', Jefferson says through stutters.

He struggles to string words together, and rubs his forehead trying to remember.

'I don't feel too good', he repeats.

'Do you mind grabbing him some water before he keels over?', Otis asks Miranda.

She does not seem eager to obey commands, and rather reluctantly heads towards the kitchen. Jefferson flops down on the sofa. Daphne guides Otis to the corner of the room, as far away from Jefferson as possible.

'What do you think?', she asks.

Otis studies the lanky figure of Jefferson that is slouched across the sofa in an ungainly manner; like everyone here, he had the opportunity but what his motive would have been eludes Otis.

'Jefferson was drunk enough to not remember much of last night. Question is, what else could he have done that he can't remember?', Otis whispers, looking in the direction of the sheath.

'Gosh, so you think that Jefferson staggered into the bar in search of more booze, and found Kiki there who made some smart remark that tipped Jefferson over the edge? So, in a drunken rage he grabbed his knife from its sheath, slit his throat. But he was so out of it, that in a panic he threw the knife somewhere and then forgot about the sheath. He then quickly shoved it down the side of the chair before everyone came back. Then downed a load more whiskey and proceeded to forget he is the murderer?', Daphne says animatedly, and without pausing for breath.

Otis looks confounded as Daphne pants for air; he begins to understand why she loves reading crime fiction so much.

'Ever thought of writing your own murder mysteries?', he says.

'I always lose interest once I know how it ends, which means writing the mysteries is a bit of a no-go for me', she says. 'By the way, if my theory is right, you owe me dinner.'

Otis smiles before quickly resuming his stern expression. He curses himself for allowing these moments of lightness with Daphne to penetrate through such a dark, sombre situation.

'The phones and power are still out. I'm going to head out to the next village. I'll probably get there quicker than Miranda's husband will get here. The weather has cleared as well. Hopefully I can flag someone down before I get there if I'm lucky', Otis says.

'I should come. Or maybe we all should?' Daphne says.

Otis places a comforting hand on her shoulder. For a moment, Daphne felt almost compelled to move in for a full hug. Instead, she stands there awkwardly wondering why she was overcome by such a thought.

'Best you stay here. Safety in numbers', he says.

'Oh yes. Very reassuring', she says nervously.

Besides I'm not sure Jefferson could actually manage the walk, looking at the state of him,' Otis continues.

'I don't know how I feel about being left here', Daphne says.

'Best thing you can do is whoever you're talking to, sound like you agree with them. Sound sympathetic. Don't challenge. Don't accuse', Otis says.

Daphne looks affronted by this advice.

'Basically, don't antagonise anyone in case they are a murderer', she says.

Otis half-smiles.

'I thought you said the chances of the murderer sticking around are slim', Daphne repeats, remembering his lack of reply to this very question last night.

Otis begins to doubt whether he should leave her. He wants to leave as big a group here as possible, to minimise the risk of anything else happening. He looks at the strangers; a fragile Jefferson who would struggle to walk the whole way, an exhausted Miranda who he doubts would be able to keep up with his pace. Confident that he will be quicker on his own, Otis presses ahead with his plan.

'I best go. We need to get help here and this may be the quickest way. Miranda's husband may return sooner than me but it's best to cover all bases', Otis says.

'You can't leave without at least telling me if you think someone here is the suspect?', Daphne persists.

Otis ponders this for a moment. Did anyone strike him as being the murderer? Not immediately. Although he sensed, at times, that there was a puppeteer. Some time alone to clear is head is much needed.

'I don't know. Something isn't quite adding up and my head feels too foggy to decipher what it is. Of course, we had those strange knocks at the door too. Was someone outside watching us? Was someone specifically watching Kiki? Waiting for him to be the one who answered the door?', Otis says.

Daphne and Otis stare at each other, deep in thought; their minds busy processing all this information and what it could mean.

'It seems odd for the sheath of the knife to be hidden separately from the knife itself. It makes me both suspect and eliminate Jefferson. It's perplexing really', Otis continues, spilling his thoughts out loud.

Miranda appears and plonks a glass of water down near Jefferson, who does not react. He remains seated on the sofa, staring blankly towards the window and paying no attention to anyone else.

'Miranda, are you sure you don't recognise it?', Otis asks, pointing at the sheath.

Miranda glances down at it again. The distinctive ruby red colour and gold stitching shimmers slightly in the light.

'No, it's not from here', she replies.

Otis looks back at Jefferson, who appears to be completely out of it, either through stress or lack of sleep, Otis assumes.

'Jefferson are you okay?', Otis asks.

Jefferson squeezes his eyes shut.

'I just want this nightmare to end. I want to get out of here', he replies.

He opens his eyes abruptly and looks at Otis.

'I'll walk to the next village. I'll be glad to leave you lot here', Jefferson says.

Otis is reluctant to let anyone leave. He may currently suspect no one in particular but everyone is still a suspect. He does not entirely trust Jefferson not to make a run for it and leave them without help.

'Perhaps you should wait for my husband to get back home?', Miranda suggests.

Otis pulls on his jacket; he reckons if he walks briskly, he could reach Dillingford in an hour or so, aided by the daylight and calmer weather.

'No. I'm going to head out now', Otis says, 'Stay together. Jefferson, that includes you. I know you're eager to leave but I'll be quicker on my own. Trust me. You're not well anyway.'

'Wait', Daphne calls.

Otis watches Daphne fumble to open her bag. She rummages through it, muttering to herself about how much she loathes her disorganisation.

'Aha! Here it is', she says.

She pulls out a small object, and unintentionally a few other items tumble out in its wake; a packet of tissues, multiple lip balms, and a sleek card wallet. Fortunately, the knickers remain inside. Otis scoops down to assist, picking up the stray objects from the floor and places them on the table.

'Sorry always a cluts', she says, 'I just wanted to give you this.'

She hands Otis a slightly squished, pitiful looking Snickers bar.

'Energy for the journey', she says.

Otis takes it, looking a little bashful.

'Don't you have a rough that time you expect your husband?', Daphne asks Miranda.

Miranda begins to rub the side of her neck, as if she has an itch. Daphne notices her body language change; her shoulders become rigid.

'It's hard to say. He'll be back sometime this morning. He does what he wants', Miranda says, looking a little bitter and ashamed.

Otis and Daphne say nothing, but both sense she is nervous about her husband.

'When you say, "he does what he wants", what do you mean?', Daphne says delicately.

Miranda walks away from them, towards the other side of the room, still rubbing her neck. Daphne watches on with concern.

'I really should go', Otis says.

'What if you're the murderer, and you're just escaping. We'll be waiting for help that never arrives. Therefore, I need to come', Jefferson says, getting up unsteadily from the chair.

'So, you want to walk a few miles in the middle of nowhere on your own with me, because you think I'm a murderer?', Otis says.

Jefferson looks puzzled. He blinks rapidly, trying to figure out what to do next. He slowly sits back down.

'Very good. Right, now I really must go. Daphne my number is written down on that piece of tissue, should the phones miraculously start working again. Not that I have charge, but I'll try to get some as soon as I can', Otis says.

He rushes out the door before Daphne has time to respond. She suddenly feels very alone.

Otis pauses at the bottom of the stairs, realising he has not seen Muhsen yet this morning. He looks up towards the landing but sees no movement; he hears the sound of a door closing but it is beyond the initial two bedrooms within his sight. It is perhaps the sound of the bathroom door, Otis considers. He is eager to get going, and instead calls out to the others.

'Fill Muhsen in when he comes down', Otis calls out to the group in the living room, as he hurries down the hallway and out through the back door.

Daphne hears the door close, but her attention is now fixed on Miranda.

'Miranda, is everything okay between you and your husband? I'm sorry if that's too personal, you just seem a little jumpy suddenly', Daphne asks gently.

Miranda slowly walks back to Daphne; she looks up at her through jaded eyes.

'He's a good man. He just gets jealous. Has a bit of a temper. But he goes off to cool down, and then comes back as good as new', Miranda says.

Daphne wants to talk about it further but is stopped from doing so by Miranda.

'I don't wish to talk about it', she says firmly.

Daphne retreats, not wishing to cause any more aggro.

'I'm sorry', Miranda says unexpectedly. 'Life has changed a great deal over the last few years. I seem to live quite a lonely and isolated life these days.'

Daphne finds herself feeling sorry for the landlady; she feels as if she should hug her but suspects that Miranda is not the hugging type.

'I didn't mean to pry', Daphne says.

Miranda dithers. Daphne can tell she is torn.

'What happened to your husband?', Miranda asks.

Daphne was not ready for this subject change. Now it is she who falters; unable to choose the words she wishes to speak. The silence has gone on for too long now not to offer Miranda some sort of satisfactory reply.

'I don't know. His death has always been classed as inconclusive', Daphne says. 'He died whilst abroad so… I wasn't with him.'

Regret twists around her gut. *If only I had gone,* she thinks. It is a thought that follows her every day, and will likely remain until her death.

Miranda seems at a loss for words.

'Inconclusive?', she repeats back to Daphne

She is not keen to give Miranda too much more information.

'I think they felt someone could have had a hand in his death but could never prove it', she replies.

Miranda looks intrigued. Daphne can tell she wants more.

'It's not something I talk about', she says.

Daphne scoops up the tissues and lip balm, and stuffs them back into her bag.

'Don't forget your card holder', Miranda says.

Daphne glances down at the remaining object on the table.

'Oh, that's not mine', she replies.

'Isn't it? But if fell from your bag', Miranda says.

Daphne's face contorts.

'But it's not mine', Daphne reaffirms.

Miranda picks up the small card holder and takes a look at it; she pulls out the ID card.

'Oh, it's Muhsen's. Weird. How did it get in your purse?', Miranda asks.

'It didn't', Daphne says, feeling befuddled by the whole conversation. 'I mean, I didn't see it fall out – perhaps you're mistaken.'

'Actually, did either of you see Muhsen earlier? He seems to be taking a while to come down', Daphne asks.

Miranda shakes her head.

'When I passed by his bedroom, I assumed he was still sleeping. Being so angry all the time probably takes it out of you', Miranda says in a mocking tone.

Daphne ignores that last remark.

'I'll go check on him', Daphne says heading out into the hall towards the staircase.

'No offence, but I don't think I'll ever invite a group of strangers to stay again', Miranda calls out, folding her arms tightly around her.

She stands in the doorway of the living room, unsure whether to stay or go with Daphne. Jefferson remains quiet, still staring into space, no doubt nursing a hangover.

Chapter 7
Smoky Fish

"To seek the truth in lies, is to seek the light in darkness."

Jefferson grips the arm of the sofa with his hand; his knuckles are as white as his face. No longer content to sit quietly, he jumps up and storms past a dubious looking Miranda. Hearing his footsteps thump up the stairs, she quickly follows, unsure what his intentions are.

'I thought we were all meant to stay together and wait?', Jefferson demands angrily, bursting into the bedroom where Daphne is stood.

Daphne jumps at his unexpected, loud arrival. A feeling of dread rises up in her.

'Muhsen?', Miranda calls, following Jefferson quickly through the door into the bedroom.

Miranda joins Daphne who is currently standing at the side of the bed, clutching a piece of paper in her hand.

'What's going on? Where is he?', Miranda asks.

'I… I have no idea. I came to find him, and he's gone', Daphne says.

'Gone?', Miranda says, walking around the bed as if to make sure he is not hiding somewhere.

Jefferson leans against the wall at the bottom of the bed; still feeling a little unsteady on his feet. He stares at the vacant bed through bloodshot eyes.

'Wait, what's that?', Miranda asks, pointing towards the paper in Daphne's hands.

'Oh, it's a note I found placed on the bed. I can't quite make it out without my glasses', Daphne says, handing it to Miranda.

She reads it out loud:

'I'll be long gone by the time you read this. You won't find me. It may mean nothing but I'm sorry for what I did.'

Daphne plays the words over and over in her head. She has no idea if it is Muhsen's handwriting, nor if it sounds like him.

'Shit. So, it was him. Unbelievable. What a nutjob – what did he even have against Kiki? They barely knew each other', Jefferson says.

Daphne scans the room; there is no sign to suggest he had spent the night here, except for the handwritten note. Miranda sits on the end of the bed and places her face in her hands.

'What a horrid and strange night', Miranda mumbles through her fingers.

Feeling for the landlady's distress, Daphne places a hand on her shoulder.

'I know. I can't even believe this is all real', Daphne says, fighting back the tears.

'Maybe he planted that sheath to make someone else, like me, look guilty', Jefferson says, feeling instantly vindicated. 'Twat', he adds.

Daphne huffs in annoyance; Jefferson is doing little to make himself less irritating.

'We are assuming he did indeed write this note', Daphne says in a bid to still maintain an open mind.

Both Miranda and Jefferson stare intensely at Daphne; she finds it a little unnerving, but she rallies herself to continue.

'All I'm saying is why would Muhsen confess. It makes no sense', Daphne says.

Everyone gets lost in their own thoughts. Jefferson screws up the note and throws the note on the bed.

'I'm sorry but why are we assuming the guy who murdered Kiki was thinking logically. Maybe he had regrets and needed to confess', Jefferson says impatiently.

'I mean, I suppose it's possible he felt guilty enough to confess but not enough to stay and face the music', Daphne ponders.

Daphne picks up the note and irons it out with her hands. She pulls it close to her face trying to study the handwriting. Miranda is watching her closely.

'Wait, are these yours?', Miranda says, feeling inside her cardigan pocket.

She pulls out a pair of black rimmed spectacles.

'Yes, where did you find them?', Daphne asks, reaching enthusiastically for them.

'Outside', she replies.

'Outside?', Daphne says with surprise.

'When did you lose them?', Jefferson asks.

Daphne wipes the lenses on her jumper, and places them back on her head. She sighs with relief.

'Oh, how I have missed being able to see', she says. 'I have no idea. I must have dropped them in all the kerfuffle last night. I only noticed this morning.'

Jefferson's facial expression swiftly shifts from white to red; his manner is no longer one of fear but one of determination. He moves around the side of the room to face Daphne.

'But why would Muhsen leave without his ID? I still don't understand how it ended up in your bag', Miranda says, looking up towards Daphne.

'What do you mean? Why do you have Muhsen's ID? When did this all happen?', Jefferson says.

'When you were busy having an emotional breakdown on the sofa just now', Miranda says.

Jefferson looks displeased at this comment.

'I have no clue how Muhsen's ID came to be anywhere, I assure you', Daphne says.

Jefferson and Miranda exchange a look; one that suggests a shift in their thoughts. Daphne feels a little uncomfortable, sensing a change in atmosphere.

'So, you amazingly had Muhsen's ID. And you just so happen to be the one who came to find him first, and discover he is *missing?*', Jefferson says.

'And you also happened to be the last one to return to the living room, right before we found Kiki', Miranda adds.

'And', Jefferson says in a commanding tone, as he strides up and down, 'you were also sleeping right across the hall from Muhsen. Yet you heard nothing? Convenient.'

Daphne is horrified by the sudden accusatory tone.

'Well, by that reasoning, maybe we should fire some insinuations Jefferson's way. Mr too-drunk-to-remember, with a knife sheath shoved down the chair where he sat all night', Daphne says defensively.

Jefferson tuts.

'Sod off with your tuts!', Daphne says. 'What exactly are you implying anyway? I came up here and magically bumped Muhsen off, and hid him before you arrived? How would I possibly manage to fight him, let alone lift his body? And pray tell me, where have I hidden his body?'

They all fall silent for a moment, each calculating their next move, The peace is short lived.

'Well, whose pub are we in? Perhaps you're some psychopath who just likes to kill your customers', Jefferson says turning on Miranda, with a deranged look in his eyes.

'Hang on, are we all forgetting that we just apparently read a confession from a man who has done a runner?', Miranda refutes. 'Frankly, I think any of you lot are capable.'

The gauntlet is thrown and a storm of words erupts, with all three talking over each other; arguing their innocence and assuming one another's guilt.

Miranda steps away from the heated conversation, shaking her head. Daphne tries to muster some courage to steady her increasingly frazzled nerves. She pinches the top of her nose which has started to ache, realising she has not drunk anything for a while.

'Okay, okay! Let's take time out for a moment. Otis is getting help. The Police will be here soon. Let's just all get a cup of tea, and sit calmly', Daphne says.

'How very British', Miranda says.

'I can't stay cooped up in this place much longer', Jefferson cries.

'I know. I feel the same. But the Police will want to talk to us, we can't just leave', Daphne insists.

'Hard to relax when we all think the other is capable of murder', Miranda says dryly.

Daphne inhales deeply.

'All we need to do is sit, drink tea, and wait for help', Daphne says slowly, trying to keep a lid on her bubbling frustrations.

'And not kill each other', Miranda says.

Daphne does not appreciate the dark humour.

'Well, I'm heading for the booze', Jefferson declares, as he marches out of the room.

Miranda looks appalled by this statement, and rushes after him.

'Hang on a minute, you can't just drink all my booze', she shouts.

'Watch me', Jefferson yells back.

Their footsteps rapidly descend the stairs, Daphne presumes heading for the bar. Their voices fade into the background; the last words she hears are those of Miranda informing Jefferson to not touch the remaining brandy. Finally, there is peace, and Daphne gladly finds herself alone for a moment. She looks around the room once more, her eyes come to rest on the empty bed. *It still looks freshly made,* she thinks. She tries to imagine what Muhsen's last movements in the pub may have been.

'So, he went upstairs and waited for everyone to fall asleep. He then somehow got down the stairs, passed Otis and out through the back door without anyone noticing', she says to herself.

It's possible, she thinks. She had found Otis in a deep sleep and dreaming heavily. The doors upstairs are thick, solid wood. Daphne pulls out her Nokia phone and sets an alarm to go off in thirty seconds' time. She places it on the bed and leaves the room, shutting the door behind her. She heads into her bedroom, shuts the door and waits. Forty seconds later she can hear no alarm. *Interesting,* she mulls. Heading back into Muhsen's room, she finds the alarm ringing.

'But why leave a note? Why confess and leave? Why not just leave?', she ponders out loud.

Daphne knows that she took a while to fall asleep, and deduces that Muhsen must not have been able to escape without waiting at least a couple of hours. *But how did he escape unseen?* She spots an in-built cupboard in the corner of the room. She feels compelled to check inside it, just in case the missing piece of the jigsaw happens to be magically within. She turns the handle and pulls; it is locked. She finds herself pressing her face up against the door, unsure what it is she is hoping to hear. Nothing stirs. Taking a final walk around the room, she concedes that there are no further clues to find.

Feeling flummoxed by the whole unravelling mystery, she heads out of the door and prays Otis returns soon.

- - -

Otis winces in pain as he tries to stretch out his back as he makes his way down the single-track lane. Much to his amazement he is greeted by signs of life much sooner than he anticipated; there, at the entrance of a winding dirt track, is a sign that reads 'Honeydew Farm'. He pauses to assess the best route. He cannot see the farm from the road, but the dirt track looks recently used. *Strange, Miranda never mentioned her farmer neighbour,* Otis thinks. *What's that sound?* He strains his ears. It appears to be coming from the direction of the dirt track.

'That's a voice I'm sure', Otis says excitably.

The track is bendy and shielded by trees, making it difficult for Otis to spot anyone. He heads as quickly as he can down the track, eager to get some help and hopeful this may be the fastest way. *I'm sure I heard a voice,* he thinks. The terrain is uneven and muddy from last night's storm. There is nothing but a mix of trees and fields around him, and no clear view of where the track leads. He manages to stop himself from taking a tumble. A few expletives fly out of his mouth. Glancing at his watch, he wonders if he made the right decision; this track is much longer than he had anticipated.

He hears a chorus of footsteps and rustling branches behind him. He turns around quickly but jars his back, sending it into spasm. He lets out a cry of anguish. He sees some sheep bustle past him, passing from one field to the other via the track.

'Blasted sheep. Thought you were the mystery murderer', he says.

Rubbing the base of his back, he cautiously takes a step forward but feels a sharp pain whip across the back of his legs, sending his body flying. He lands face down with a thud. He tries to lift himself, but it is no good. His brain forces his eyes shut and his body goes limp.

- - -

Daphne calls out for Jefferson and Miranda, unsure of their exact whereabouts. She searches in the living room, bar and kitchen. There is no sign of them. The sudden peace and quiet is not a welcome feeling to Daphne right now. *Where are they?* She heads back into the living room and looks out of the window. Craning her neck she looks to the left, out towards the small, tarmacked area in front of the pub. She sees Miranda stood on the edge of the road. She pushes open the window.

'What are you doing?', she shouts.

Miranda looks around, momentarily unsure where the voice is coming from.

'Waiting for a car to pass so I can flag it down', she calls back. 'Not that we get much traffic round here.'

It's not a bad idea, Daphne thinks.

'Just feeling desperate. And helpless. I can't sit doing nothing', Miranda continues.

'Where's Jefferson, I can't find him?', Daphne says.

Miranda does not look up; she shakes her head and waves her hand as if swotting a fly away. Daphne looks out over the rolling fields; all is still. There is no sign of any other people. No cars. No bikes. No walkers. Usually, the tranquility of the countryside brings her a sense of joy. Today it brings nothing but a foreboding feeling of fear. She shuts the window, and glances down at her watch. *Otis should reach the village soon,* she thinks.

'Jefferson?', Daphne calls.

No reply comes. Daphne folds her arms tightly, as if giving herself a reassuring hug. Despite her own insistence they should all remain calm and wait patiently, she finds herself heading back out into the bar. Her unyielding quizzical mind leads her back to Kiki, reassessing the crime scene for any unnoticed clues. She picks up the receiver of the pub phone as she passes, there is still no dial tone. She slams it back down, finding it increasingly hard not to feel enraged by the continuing isolation.

Slowly walking around the body, Daphne studies every item of furniture, every object, every tiny blemish she finds. *Nothing.* She leans against the wall near an old, wooden sideboard by the door. *This detective lark is harder than it looks,* she thinks. Staring blankly at a porcelain hare that sits proudly on top of the unit, Daphne's eyes lose focus as her mind drifts into a daze. That is until something captures her eye. A flash of silver.

'What's that?'

She stretches her fingers to reach down the back of the sideboard, trying to ignore the intrusive thoughts telling her a spider is lurking behind there. The idiocy of being more afraid of a spider than an actual killer escapes her. Daphne touches something cold and metal, with some sort of screen. It appears to be taped to the back of the unit. Pulling her hand free, she looks around to check that no one is there, before gently pulling the sideboard out from the wall fractionally. She squeezes her eyes in confusion, as she tries to work out what is taped there and why. Pulling it free from its tape prison, she quickly pushes the unit back into place and studies the device. It appears to be a silver Dictaphone. She turns it over and finds a smooth metallic label stuck to the back with the words:

M. Bashar

'Daphne?'

Daphne quickly shoves the device in her pocket, and follows the sound of Miranda's voice calling out to her. She looks through the window by the front entrance, and much to her joy she sees a vehicle outside. Overcome with anticipation, she rushes out of the room down the hallway and through the back door. Rounding the corner, she sees a rather striking, tall man step out of the vehicle. Miranda is talking at speed; some of what she says sounds like gibberish; sentences tumble out of her mouth like a landslide of words.

'We desperately need some help. There's a... a... -', Miranda is stopped abruptly by the handsome stranger.

'Don't worry. Take a few deep breaths. Why don't you show me what the problem is?', the man says calmly.

Daphne is struck by how serene the man is.

'Not much makes me skittish', he says, as if reading Daphne's mind.

Daphne feels the Dictaphone in her pocket; she desperately wants to hit the play button. *Could it have recorded Kiki's last moments? Why was it there? Did Kiki place it there knowing he was about to be confronted by someone? He was a poet so possessing a Dictaphone would not be surprising.* These questions raced through her mind, drowning out the words being spoken between Miranda and the man.

'So, you both live here?', the man asks.

'I do. I'm Miranda, the Landlady.'

'Oh, I'm not from round here. Train got cancelled so a group of us got stranded. Otis, one of the other passengers, has walked to the next village to find help. And Jefferson-', Daphne looks around, 'well he was here but I can't find him.'

Daphne feels concerned; it is unlike Jefferson to not be visible. Or vocal.

'They still running trains to Dillingford? Didn't think any stopped there anymore', the man says.

'Think that'll soon be the case', Miranda replies.

'Not surprised. Like a ghost town in some of these parts now', the man reflects glumly.

'But… but cancelled trains are the least of our worries. Something terrible has happened', Miranda pauses to compose herself, she wipes her forehead with a tissue from her pocket. 'The two other random people who turned up at my pub, well, one was killed last night. And the other, well he has done a runner – apparently because he did it',

Miranda places her hand across her mouth, shocked by the story she has had to tell. The man gasps, unsure whether this is all a hoax. He flips between laughing and grimacing, as he tries to deduce if this is all a joke.

'You're kidding?', he cries.

Miranda lowers her head and shakes it slowly.

'I wish I was. It's been horrendous the last few hours', she replies.

The man still appears unsure what to do, he shifts his stance numerous times and fidgets with his coat sleeves. Daphne is unable to rid herself of the thought that something is amiss with Jefferson's sudden absence. The man and Miranda watch Daphne head to the back door and call out for Jefferson. When no response comes, she walks back towards them looking disoriented.

'He can't just vanish. Do you have a signal on your phone?', Daphne asks the man.

'No, the nearest place you'll start to get some signal is the small village of Dillingford', the man replies.

'Why on earth would they put a train station in such a stupid spot', Daphne says, losing her cool.

'Well, when they built it they thought Dillingford was going to be expanding rapidly. But that all fell through-'

Miranda interrupts the man.

'I'm sorry, but shouldn't we focus on what we're going to do next', Miranda says.

'Er... yeah of course. Sorry. Let's find that Jefferson bloke and then head into town for help', the man responds.

They enter the pub, still calling out for Jefferson. There is no sign. The man moves around the new surroundings with caution, and observes his new companions. As they come to a stop just shy of reaching Kiki's body, he becomes distracted by something.

'You got blood on your shoe', the man says to Miranda.

Both Daphne and Miranda look down at her cream pumps. There is a streak of red across one of them.

'What the hell!? That wasn't there earlier', Miranda cries.

'Have you been near Kiki's body?', Daphne asks.

'No, why would I go near that? How do you know it's even blood?', Miranda says.

'Well, I guess there's a chance it could be something else. It sure looks like blood to me. Unless you've been eating ketchup?', the man says.

Daphne is not sure whether the last bit was a joke. The man remains pokerfaced; Daphne assumes it was not.

'So, you were the last one to see this Jefferson fella, were you?', the man says, looking curiously at Miranda.

Daphne's mind suddenly floods with new suspicions. *What if something bad has happened to Jefferson?,* she thinks. She stares at the blood-flecked trainer.

'Jefferson!', Daphne screams out, one final time.

All three of them wait for something to happen. Nothing does. All is quiet. All is still.

'Did you do something to him?', Daphne asks Miranda.

Miranda looks at her in disbelief. She could not open her mouth any wider even if she wanted to.

'I can't believe you're asking me that! So now you think that I somehow bumped Jefferson off and managed to hide him all in the ten minutes before you came back downstairs', Miranda says, looking vexed by the sudden shift in suspicion.

'Not pleasant to be accused of things, is it?', Daphne says resentfully. 'And when you suggested I had something to do with all this, I didn't even have blood on my shoe.'

The man takes a few steps away from them; his calmness is interrupted by a flicker of worry as he spots the sheet drenched in red on the floor, and the outline of a body beneath it. He clutches his throat, Daphne wonders if he is going to be sick.

'Er... this is all too much. I think it's best I go get some help', the man says.

'I thought we were coming with you?', Miranda asks.

The man takes a couple of more steps, trying to move back towards the hallway.

'Maybe it's best I go alone', he says, looking unsure of himself.

'No wait!', Daphne cries. 'I just need two minutes. I need to go, um... to the toilet.'

They both stop and look at her, unsure why she announced this so emphatically. Daphne wishes to waste no more time, and quickly spins around and heads to the cloakroom. She must know what is on the Dictaphone; it may tell her everything she needs to know. She ignores the distant cry of Miranda asking her to explain herself.

Bolting the door, she sits on the toilet lid and pulls out the device; her hands are shaking. Her pulse quickens. She hits the rewind button and plays it from the start. There is nothing but silence. Daphne waits. Still nothing. Her finger hovers over the fast forward button, but she resists in case she misses the slightest of sounds. Daphne places the Dictaphone on the side, and rests her head in the cup of her hand. The minutes tick by. She feels an increasing disappointment. This feeling is soon shattered by a very loud sound:

Knock-knock-knock

Daphne jumps. She stares at the cloakroom door, caught unawares by such loud knocks being hammered against the wood. Her ears ring from the sudden explosion of noise.

'I just need a minute', Daphne calls out.

She listens, but no response comes. Daphne returns her attention to the Dictaphone. It had been playing for over 6 minutes and nothing had happened. Overcome with impatience she fast forwards by 60 seconds. Then another. Then another. Twelve minutes in, her hopes have all but faded of anything significant happening.

Knock-knock-knock

Daphne jumps again at the exact same sound. Daphne stares at the cloakroom door, and then back down at the Dictaphone.

'Wait a minute', she says.

She hits rewind for a few seconds, lowers the volume, and then plays it once again.

Knock-knock-knock

Her mouth drops open. *The door knocks were fake,* she thinks. *That's why they were so damn loud.*

'Mother of cows!', she cries.

'Daphne?', Miranda calls out.

'Where are you? We all heard knocking?', the man says.

'Crap!', Daphne says under –her breath, as she hastily pushes the Dictaphone back into her pocket.

Unbolting the door, she is greeted by Miranda and the man.

'Ah yes, the knocking. That was just me, testing a theory. Um… just wanted to see how hard I… um, had to knock for you to hear it', Daphne says.

'What theory is this?', the man asks.

Daphne swallows heavily, realising she has a significant piece of evidence that will help solves the case. *This means that someone in the group did it; an inside job,* she thinks. She eyes Miranda with a newfound loathing. *My new*

109

suspect numero uno. Daphne remembers the sticker on the back of the Dictaphone. *M. Bashar.*

'Well, whilst you faff around with your theories, I'm going to check on something' Miranda says, hurrying out towards the bar.

'Check on what?', Daphne calls out to her.

She is blocked from following her by the man.

'Now, Daphne. This is obviously a very horrid situation. Miranda's explained it a little more to me whilst we were waiting for you', he says.

'Oh, I bet she has', Daphne says feistily.

The man pauses and blinks rapidly.

'Are you okay?', he asks.

'You mean aside from the fact that there's a murdered man in the next room?', Daphne replies.

'Um… yes. Well, I need to get the Police here. We need to go together and get this sorted out', he says.

She nods her head, feeling slightly dazed from the sudden overload of thoughts racing through her mind. Daphne feels a smidge of guilt that she, not only disturbed the crime scene, but stole from it. *Perhaps I'll tell him,* she thinks, eager to share with someone what she has discovered, desperately needing to hear someone else's theory and see if it aligns with her own, or if this whole situation is making her lose all rational thinking.

'The thing is, I think I've found something. A piece of evidence', Daphne says.

The man looks intrigued. He presses her for more information but Daphne finds herself unable to focus, not knowing what Miranda is currently doing or where she is.

'Let's find Miranda, and then talk privately', she says.

She bustles past the man and walks quickly through the pub to locate Miranda; the man is hot on her heels.

'I wasn't expecting any of this. I was just heading to have breakfast with my little boy', the man says sadly. 'I don't get to see him much.'

'I know. I'm sorry you've been dragged into this', Daphne says. 'But I'm glad you're here.'

There is no sign of Miranda in the living room. Daphne picks up her backpack, knocking Muhsen's ID off the table. She picks it up, automatically glancing at the ID card in the clear pocket as she places it back down. Had it not been for his name, she would not have recognised Muhsen from his picture. His hair is much shorter, and he is clean shaven. Heading back towards the man, she comes to a halt.

'Wait a minute', she says.

The man looks puzzled.

She runs back and picks up the ID.

'Muhsen Bashir', she cries.

'Erm… what's going on?', the man says, looking increasingly nervous.

Daphne desperately needs a few moments to think; to put all these fragments together.

'Come on, let's find Miranda quickly', she says, rushing past the man.

They soon find her in the kitchen, rigorously trying to wipe the blood from her shoe with a Brillo pad. Miranda appears desperate to rid herself of the stain, which only adds to Daphne's growing state of confusion and paranoia.

'Hey!', Daphne cries, suddenly feeling angry.

Miranda turns towards her, ready to fire off some rebuttal but she is quickly derailed by the sight of something behind Daphne.

'Oh my god! Daphne look behind you!', she cries.

Chapter 8
Beginning of the End

"We never truly know anyone, not even ourselves."

'Detective Hurt, you need to let this go. You did all you could', Superintendent Richmond said.

Otis felt an anger light a fire inside him like never before. He launched his bag across the room, it hit the chair and sent one of the buttons flying. Richmond looked stunned, unsure what to do for a moment.

'You need to get a hold of yourself, Detective Hurt', Richmond said.

Otis wiped a bead of sweat from his forehead, and slowly picked up his bag and button. He sat down on the hard, black chair in the interview room and buried his head in his hand. Richmond watched on, sensing that he was witnessing the final days of Otis being a detective.

'Why this case of all cases?', Richmond asked.

Otis looked up, his face red with frustration.

'I made a promise to a young girl that the man who took her parents from her would see justice. I promised that I would find him, and make sure he got put behind bars', he said.

'That was some promise', Richmond said.

Otis rubbed his temples with his fingers; his head throbbed from exhaustion and dehydration.

'Is that not a standard promise any detective would make?', Otis asked.

Richmond took a seat. He studied the man in front of him; a man who had probably been one of the most accomplished detectives under his watch.

'You've got a lion's heart you know that', Richmond said.

Otis half chuckled.

'A lion's heart but a kitten's bite', he replied.

Otis reached into his bag and pulled out a sealed envelope. He pushed it across the table towards Richmond.

'I think you know what this is; and I think you know I have to do this', Otis said.

'You don't have to resign,' Richmond said.

Otis looked up at Richmond; he could see the regret in his eyes.

'I do. Because by the time I have finished trying to bring that man to justice, you'd have to fire me anyway', Otis said.

'Why? What are you planning to do?', Richmond asked with an air of concern.

Otis stood up and gathered his things.

'Goodbye, Sir', he said, before swiftly leaving.

Otis's soul feels heavy from this memory that forever plagues his dreams. He is unsure if he has been unconscious or drifting in and out of reality. He has a splitting headache, and his whole body vibrates in pain. Having lost all concept of time, he scrambles for his phone.

'Are you okay, mate?', an unfamiliar voice says.

Otis can make out a blurry figure of a man standing over him. He tries to stand up but his knees sting from scraped skin.

'Hold up a minute, let me help', the man says.

Otis feels a firm hand grip his arm and pull him up.

'Where am I? What happened?', Otis asks, feeling a rising sense of anxiety.

'Looks like you took a tumble mate. I hope my animals had nothing to do with it', the man says.

Otis realises he is being watched by a circle of curious sheep.

'I'm Lee.'

'Otis', he replies, still trying to get an unblurred vision of the man that is helping him; his eyes need a moment to adjust.

He tries to remember what he had been doing before the fall; everything feels muddled.

'I'm not sure what happened', Otis says.

The back of his leg throbs.

'I don't know if something hit me from behind?', Otis says, feeling the back of his shins which are stinging.

'I bet it was bloody Bella', Lee says.

Otis looks up at him completely perplexed.

'Her', Lee says, pointing towards one of the sheep.

'She's a right shifty bugger. Charges at your legs when you're not looking', Lee says.

Otis stares at the innocent looking sheep.

'Oh dear, looks like this is the real casualty,' Lee says, handing Otis the crushed Snickers bar that had fallen on the floor.

All of a sudden, Otis is hit with the memory of Kiki, The King's Feet, and Daphne.

'Lee, I need to speak to the Police. I need them to go to The King's Feet – a man was killed there', Otis says, sending his heart racing.

'Take it easy, you still don't look too good. You may have concussion', Lee responds.

Otis looks down at his watch and is horrified to discover the face has been smashed. The last and only heirloom he has of his father. It had survived decades of police chases, and countless travels across the world; yet this is how it ends. Smashed by a sheep. He does not have time to process the pain of the last remembrance he has left of his father being shattered; he shakes off the pain and tries to refocus.

'What? Um… what time is it? How long have I been down for?', Otis says, still feeling jumbled.

'It is about 7.30ish', Lee says.

Otis's jaw drops. He has lost around an hour. A sudden shiver surges through his entire body; the after-effect of lying on the cold ground for so long takes hold. His sodden trousers cling to the skin around his kneecaps.

'Maybe we best get you to the hospital', Lee suggests.

Otis moves with care towards a nearby fence and leans against it. He gives himself a moment; steadily his senses awaken, and his usual calm logic begins to emerge.

'Do you have network on your phone?', Otis asks hopefully.

'Nope, sorry. You get network in Dillingford, but for some reason round here it's always been an issue', Lee says.

'Appreciate this will all sound very radical, but a few passengers and I were stranded at the pub as our train got cancelled due to the storm. One of the passengers was murdered last night; we found him with his throat slit. I left to find help once last night's storm had cleared as the power has been out since yesterday. We need to at least get to Dillingford, and phone for help', Otis pleads.

Lee looks pensively at him; he scratches his nose numerous times. His eyes narrow, and a crease emerges in his forehead like a lightning bolt. He studies Otis carefully.

'You're telling me someone was actually murdered at that pub down the road?', Lee says, aghast.

Otis nods.

'Always thought the pub looked a bit creepy in recent years', Lee says.

'I know it sounds horrifying, but we need to get the Police to the pub pronto', Otis pleads again.

Lee resumes scratching his nose thoughtfully, trying to decide what part he should play in this.

'Alright. But don't you think we should check whether they've managed to call for help whilst you've been away', Lee suggests.

'I, um… maybe', Otis stumbles over his words. 'I don't want to waste more time, that's the thing.'

'They may well have got the phone line working, and got help. Let's head back there first it's just two minutes down the road in my truck', Lee says.

Otis still feels woozy from his fall, and chooses to go along with Lee's suggestion; so long as there was a plan, and it involved them going somewhere. The thought of checking on Daphne also seems to bring him comfort. Otis begins to walk slowly back down the track, being extra careful with every step he takes. Lee ushers the remaining sheep into one of the fields and shuts the gate. Feeling unsteady on his feet, Otis pauses to get his bearings.

'Wait up. Where do you think you're going?', Lee says, catching up with Otis. 'I'll walk down the track and get my truck, you sit here. It'll take me about 20 minutes or so but just stay put.'

Otis is not too happy. Yet more time is being lost as he stands around being useless.

'Hang on, you said it would just be two minutes to get to the pub', Otis cries.

'Yeah. Once I get my truck. Either way, we need to add on twenty minutes for me to get the truck before we go anywhere', Lee says.

Otis tries to steady his breathing, and quell his ever-increasing frustration.

'You won't be able to walk quick enough to get to the truck yourself in under twenty minutes. We'll have to add on forty minutes if you want to tag along', Lee insists.

Otis begrudgingly leans against a nearby field wall, he raises his hand up in defeat. His body had spoken.

'Fine, fine. Please hurry', Otis says.

Lee hightails it down the winding track, Otis soon loses sight of him. Feeling around his pockets, Otis pulls out his dead phone. He feels completely cut off from the world, totally at the mercy of a stranger's kindness. Otis closes his eyes, and continues to try to steady his breathing, and ignore the pain he is in. The sun peeps out of the clouds briefly, and the feeling of warmth hitting his body brings a sense of healing and rejuvenation. As Otis waits, he finds himself gradually becoming blissfully lost in the peace of his surroundings. Such peace in his life had been rare. Throughout his life he has felt like death has followed him; he wonders if that is all he will ever know.

The stillness is broken by the sound of a truck engine approaching. Otis has no idea how long he has been waiting. Having no watch and no phone is both liberating and debilitating.

'Right, hop in', Lee shouts.

Otis has never been so relieved to see a truck. He clambers in, with a little help. And squeezes into the cramped space available. As nice as it is to not be walking, the lack of the suspension and bumpy road makes Otis feel like his brain is being rattled.

'So, what are we expecting to walk into?', Lee asks.

'Well, I'm not sure. Either a very stressed, frustrated group of people who have been waiting for me to return with help, or they managed to get some help and we find an active crime scene with Police presence. I'm hoping for the latter', Otis says.

'And um… well are any of these frustrated people also a potential murderer?', Lee asks cautiously.

'That is a very good question', Otis says.

'So good that it clearly doesn't have an answer', Lee quips.

Otis realises how worrisome this must be for Lee, who thought all he was doing was helping a man who fell. Now he finds himself heading towards the scene of a murder. He wishes he could give more detail, but all his energy is being used to keep him from being sick as the motion of the truck tests his resilience. Otis has never craved his bed so desperately as he does right now.

'I really appreciate your help', Otis says.

Lee gives a nod of acknowledgment. As they turn off the farm track and onto the much smoother lane. Otis is relieved by the shift to a smoother ride.

'It's so quiet round here', Otis observes.

The undulating fields span for miles, a mix of gold and green as far as the eye can see.

'Yeah, since they built the by-pass hardly anyone uses this road anymore, and a lot of the farms have become derelict as the generations have changed', Lee replies.

The pub comes into view; Otis strains to see if there is any sign of activity. As they edge closer, Otis feels less and less optimistic. There is no sign of a police car, or police tape. Everything looks still. Lee pulls up onto the verge just before the entrance to the pub. They both climb out of the truck.

'So do you have any suspicions about anyone in there?', Lee asks quietly.

Otis had not been anticipating such a question at this moment; he was poised to head straight towards the pub.

'To be honest, I've gone back and forth on this. But I am starting to wonder if there is only one possible scenario-'

A pheasant emerges from the bushes with a loud flutter, and flies past them. It almost catches Lee on the head as it soars by, causing both men to jump backwards. Otis loses his train of thought.

'You may regret coming back here, you know', Lee says.

'Regret? Why?', Otis asks, turning to face Lee.

He leans up into his truck and reaches behind the seat and pulls out a shotgun.

Otis's survival instincts immediately kick into gear, noting Lee's sudden grim expression.

'Listen, Lee. Let's talk. Put down the gun, and let's talk', Otis says calmly.

In a split-second Otis's mind flashes back to the trauma of six months ago:

Otis confronted the man with the menacing grin. He loathed the man's smile; how could something that represented happiness look so evil. The man holds a knife out in front of him, swishing it back and forth – threatening to use it on Otis.

'It's over. You need to give it up', Otis said.

The man laughed, a horrid booming laugh. He was mocking Otis. Taunting him. For a man missing so many teeth he certainly liked to smile.

'You really think you have anything on me? I've already been tried once. NOT GUILTY. Remember?', the man said through laughter.

'I'll make sure you're put behind bars for taking away that girl's parents', Otis said.

'Alrigh', alrigh'. I'll confess. They BEGGED me to take their life', the man said.

Otis's blood reached boiling point. Filled with anger, he lunged at the man without thinking it through. A piercing pain spread through Otis's body. The knife had torn through his skin; he could feel the warm treacle of blood running down his stomach. The man ran away.

Otis is thrust back into the present moment; he realises he has been holding his breath and releases the air from his lungs. His head feels light.

'Don't be a plank, mate. I'm not going to shoot you. Just thought, you know, with talk of murders, it may be worth having some protection', Lee says.

'When a man suddenly pulls out a gun, after you've seen a murder happen here... well, your instinct is to be on high alert', Otis says.

Lee looks at his gun and then back towards Otis.

'Yeah, perhaps I should have forewarned you', Lee says.

'Why did you say I'd regret coming back here?', Otis asks.

'Oh, I just meant if the murderer is still here or something', Lee says.

'Let's leave that locked away in the truck; we don't want any accidents', Otis suggests.

Lee looks bemused.

'But I'm a fantastic shot', he says.

Somehow this does not reassure Otis. Lee appeases him and places the gun back inside the truck.

They walk the final steps towards the pub. Otis looks into the windows anticipating seeing a face, hopefully Daphne's. No one appears.

'Seems dead', Lee says. 'Oh, no pun intended'.

Otis frowns: he wonders whether they all went on foot and are yet to return, meaning Kiki has been left inside. He heads to the window by the door and presses his face up against it. He takes a few steps back, and turns towards Lee.

'The man who was murdered, his body has gone', he says.

Lee stares back blankly.

Otis tries the front door; it is locked. He peers through another window. There is no sign of police tape or anything that suggests this had been treated as a crime scene.

'We need to find a way in', Otis says, pushing at the front door again.

'Perhaps the Police have been and gone', Lee says.

'They wouldn't have been able to get the police here, gather all the forensic evidence, remove the body and close the crime scene in the space of a couple of hours', Otis says. 'Let's try round the back.'

Otis hurries around the side of the pub; the aches in his body have faded into the background, too preoccupied with the latest puzzle pieces of this mystery. He spots the curtain in the living room is closed, except for a gap in the middle. He surreptitiously peers through. Goosebumps break out across his arms. There, in the middle of the living room, sat on a wooden chair, is Miranda. Her hands are tied up behind her back and she appears to be gagged. Otis cannot see anyone else in the room. He very slowly moves away from the window, and gestures to Lee to remain silent. Creeping slowly towards him, Otis whispers:

'The landlady is tied up. I can't see who else is in there, or who is holding her hostage. I assume it is the murderer.'

Lee starts to panic, his eyes bulge.

'What do we do? We need to run', Lee says manically.

'Shhh! Stay calm. I need you to go and get help, as fast as you can', Otis says.

'What about you?', Lee asks with apprehension.

'I need to stay here, keep an eye on things. See if I can work out who is in there', he replies. 'Go on, go quickly!'

Lee hesitates.

'Go!', Otis demands.

Lee rushes off round the corner towards the truck. Otis stays low, in case this time the sound of the truck starting alerts the hostage taker inside. He crouches down near the bushes against the wall, and tries to catch his breath. He had not been expecting this. He tries to regulate his breathing; his body is still recovering from the trauma of the earlier fall. He waits patiently until he is sure the truck has aroused no suspicions from inside. He decides to try and scope out where the others might be, and who could be behind this.

He crawls beneath the living room window, and carefully peers in again. The scene remains unchanged: Miranda is still alone, tied to the chair. Otis continues to crawl, making his way to the back of the pub and to the next window which happens to be the back door. He takes a deep breath, readying himself; craning his neck he slowly peers in but there is no sign of anyone. He continues to crawl to the window on the other side of the pub. Once again, he braces himself before raising his head up to look inside. Nothing.

'Bugger', he says under his breath.

Despite his stealthy sneaking, he is none the wiser. He wonders where Daphne could be. *What if she's being tortured? What if she's being killed? What if she's dead?*, he thinks. The image of the little girl tugging at his arm and asking him why he let the man get away, flashes into his mind. Otis slaps his head.

'Go away', he mutters.

He decides he cannot sit idly by whilst someone is in danger; he could not live with another nightmare haunting his dreams. He heads towards the back door, and very slowly tries the handle. It is locked. Otis looks up at the windows, only one is open and it is, he assumes, for the upstairs bathroom. He rushes over towards the tired looking garage, keeping hunched over in an attempt to remain as inconspicuous as possible.

The garage door is ajar; he peeps in. An old red sports car is parked inside. It looks familiar. *Perhaps Miranda's husband has returned?*, Otis thinks. He very slowly edges the garage door open, and squeezes inside. He studies the car wondering why it looks so familiar.

'Damn. That's the car that nearly ran us over the other night', he mutters.

Thoughts continue to flood Otis's mind. *What if Miranda is the murderer and they tied her up? What if it is her husband? But why move Kiki's body? Where are the others?*

He scours the garage looking for anything that may help him. Aside from some old paint cans the only other item in here is a ladder. He stares at it, wondering how reckless it would be to actually try and climb into the open window and not get seen. Daphne's face appears in his mind.

'Sod it', he says, as he grabs the ladder and throws caution to the wind.

Trying to sneak back across the courtyard with a ladder proves more difficult than he had anticipated. His eyes move around frantically as he obsessively looks at every window to ensure he is not being watched. His back groans from the weight and awkwardness of carrying the ladder. Otis positions it as delicately as he can against the wall. With one final glance around, he begins to climb. Reaching the window, he looks in; unsure what to expect. The bathroom appears empty. *Thank goodness.* The window sits directly above the bath, making it a little easier for Otis to climb down from the windowsill. He softly lands in the bath in a very uncomfortable, contorted position. He remains there for a moment, listening for any movement. Nothing. The bathroom is sparse, there are no towels or toiletries as far as he can see.

He opens the door as carefully as he can, praying it does not creak or squeak. He hovers again, listening for any sounds. He then proceeds to tip toe down the landing; he barely draws breath for fear of someone hearing him. Each of the bedroom doors is open; each time he passes one he carefully glances inside. All seems still.

He is almost at the top of the stairs, with one final door to pass. Something catches his eye this time though, an object on the floor near the entrance to the final bedroom. Checking his surroundings, he approaches the item. It is a phone; he scoops down to pick it up and taps the screen, but the battery must have died. He recognises the phone though, it is Muhsen's; he is only able to identify it as his as he was always glued to it. *Odd for Muhsen to leave his phone behind,* Otis thinks. He feels it is unlikely that Muhsen willingly left it.

Otis puts the phone in one of his pockets, and gives a final glance around the room. He then heads back out to the landing, and lightly makes his way down the stairs. As he nears the bottom, he can see the living room door is open. There is still no other movement in the pub.

'Mmmm!', Otis hears Miranda cry feebly, constricted by the cotton cloth shoved between her teeth.

Otis reaches the living room door, and peers around the frame. Miranda spots him, her eyes come alive. Otis enters quietly and pulls the gag from her mouth, encouraging her to stay quiet.

'Who did this?', he says.

Miranda sobs.

'They killed him', she says, barely audible

'They? Who?', Otis says. 'I'll get you out of here, don't worry.'

'I don't think you will', she says.

Otis looks behind him, and finds Jefferson standing in the doorway holding a pair of handcuffs. His eyes look red and recently emptied of tears.

'Jefferson?', Otis says.

Jefferson says nothing; he throws the pair of handcuffs onto the sofa next to where Otis is stood.

'You need to put those on', Jefferson says coldly.

'Do I? And what if I don't?', Otis says.

'Then Daphne dies because of you', he replies.

Otis is stunned by this response. *Could Jefferson really be the killer?*, Otis thinks. He cannot see if Jefferson is armed in any way; although Otis knows he could have something concealed, and so keeps his distance for now. Jefferson moves his hand towards his pocket, suggesting he may have a weapon.

'Tell me where Daphne is', Otis demands.

'Do you want Daphne to end up like Kiki', Jefferson says angrily.

Otis stares into Jefferson's eyes; he never thought they were the eyes of a killer. *Was I mistaken?*, he thinks. *Can we ever really truly tell?*

'The thing is, Jefferson, why would I put those handcuffs on willingly? I could simply overpower you and find Daphne', Otis says.

'You could potentially overpower me. But you would never locate Daphne; and that's a promise. It's up to you whether you want her blood on your hands. If you think you can live with that, go ahead', Jefferson says.

'You also look injured', he adds, bringing his argument to an abrupt close.

Otis notices Jefferson's whole body is shaking; he cannot tell if it is the buzz of adrenaline or pure fear. Otis glances at Miranda, who shakes her head.

'Please just do as he says. Muhsen is missing too; he may have done something to him as well', Miranda pleads.

Otis looks thunderstruck.

'Jefferson, are you really telling me you killed Kiki? What have you done to Muhsen?', Otis says.

Jefferson twitches and looks away from him; he refuses to provide answers. Otis thinks back to the previous night, and the sight of Jefferson staggering back to his seat. *Was Jefferson returning from an altercation with Kiki?*, he wonders.

'I don't understand why you would want to harm Kiki', Otis says.

He slowly edges closer to Jefferson, raising his hands gently in a show of peace. Jefferson looks panicked.

'I wouldn't do that', he screams at Otis. 'You have no idea what I could do to you.'

Otis takes a few steps back again; the scar on his stomach begins to sting, as if his body is sending him a reminder of what can happen if he misjudges someone or a situation.

'Please just do as he says. I don't want to be left here alone. I don't want to see anyone else die', Miranda pleads again, turning her head towards the handcuffs on the sofa.

Otis feels unsure of himself; he is no longer the strong, confident police detective. *What right do I have to toy with people's lives?*, Otis thinks, contemplating how his next decision could mean life or death for others. Bogged down by insecurity, he succumbs to Miranda's heavy sobs and picks up the hand cuffs.

'Cuff yourself to the radiator', Jefferson demands.

Otis obliges.

'Now what?', Otis says.

Jefferson looks unsure of himself; he glances to the left of him.

'There I've done it, please let me go', Jefferson cries.

'Who are you talking to?', Otis asks.

Jefferson appears to be looking at someone in the hallway.

'Who are you talking to?', Otis demands again.

Otis can hear the faint sound of a whisper, he cannot tell if it is a male or female voice. Whatever the mysterious voice said, it prompts Jefferson to walk slowly across the room and sit on the sofa. He glances nervously at Otis.

'What is going on? You look white as a sheet; talk to me', Otis tells him.

Jefferson turns away from him, and stares towards the door with a look of fright on his face. Another figure appears in the doorway.

Otis's heart almost stops beating.

'Daphne?'

Chapter 9
The Mask

"Now you don't see me, now you do."

As soon as Otis's eyes meet Daphne's he is overcome with a strong emotion; despite what appeared to be playing out in front of him he refuses to believe Daphne could be involved with any kind of murder. Something does not feel right, as he watches Daphne peer round the door with a severe look on her face. Dark clouds have formed under her eyes, their striking emerald colour has lost its glint. She seems to have aged years within hours.

'What's going on?', Otis asks.

Daphne does not respond. She stares intensely at him, but Otis cannot read her emotionless expression. She looks frozen, unwilling or unable to give away even the slightest hint.

'Tell me what is happening?', Otis says, feeling increasingly desperate.

Otis notices Daphne is hiding her hands behind her back; she could be concealing a weapon or be restrained; he cannot tell.

'Show me your hands', Otis demands.

Daphne remains silent, and still. She avoids any further eye contact with him. Otis has a million theories rushing through his mind; in each one he refuses to have Daphne as the perpetrator.

Miranda and Jefferson keep quiet, apparently too afraid to say anything out of turn.

'For God's sake, Daphne, explain what is happening', Otis says with fading confidence.

Surely, she cannot be the mastermind behind all of this, Otis pleads inwardly.

'Okay that'll do. Put poor Otis out of his misery, will you?', a distant voice calls from beyond the living room walls.

Otis knows that voice but among the drama he is unable to place it momentarily.

Daphne slowly turns around to reveal her hands are also cuffed. Much to his shame, Otis's immediate reaction is one of relief. Relief that she is a fellow hostage, and not the hostage taker. Daphne gets pushed into the room by a looming figure of a man behind her. She flops down on the sofa next to Jefferson. Otis wants to make sure she is okay; however, his focus must remain on whoever is pulling the strings beyond the walls of the room.

'Don't feel bad, Otis, for not cracking this case', says the man.

The owner of the mystery voice steps into view.

'Lee?', Otis cries.

'Not everyone can be Sherlock', Lee says.

Lee sniggers at Otis; his previous friendly manner is replaced by pure, undiluted callousness. Lee stands towering over his prisoners, clutching his trusty shotgun. Otis flicks rapidly through every interaction he had with Lee. *What else did I miss?*

'Sorry about that whole thing with Jefferson and Daphne. I just wanted to screw with your head. I told them I'd shoot them if they didn't go along with it', Lee says, admiring his gun.

'You didn't do too badly', Lee continues, looking briefly at Jefferson and Daphne. 'Not as good as me, but not bad for a couple of sissies.'

Neither Jefferson nor Daphne respond, they turn their heads away from him not wanting to pander to his games anymore. Otis detects the faint whisper of Daphne saying sorry, perhaps selfishly, he assumes the apology is meant for him.

'So what's the plan then, Lee? Because I'm not convinced you've got a good one', Otis says.

Lee averts his gaze from his gun towards Otis instead; his eyes cease to blink, and bulge with madness. It is as if the beast within Lee has suddenly awoken. Otis wonders how he managed to conceal it; he had no inkling such a monster had come to his aid earlier. The fact that such wickedness can camouflage itself, is enough to give even the most intrepid among us nightmares.

'Cocky, aren't you? Strange, given you're the one currently handcuffed to the radiator', Lee says. 'It's a shame you swanned off for your little walk down the lane; you missed so much of the show.'

Lee continues to admire his weapon; he strokes it softly like a child would a newborn kitten. He has the look of a man who is fuelled by the excitement of using it on his next victim.

'The show?', Otis asks.

Otis sensed this word held significance. Lee leans in the doorway, posing with the gun like some sort of model. Otis can tell he is the kind of man who has managed to get away with so much, simply by virtue of his good looks. The kind of man whose downfall will be his own vanity.

'Ah yes, the show. Couldn't have done it without Bella the sheep', Lee says.

He begins laughing at Otis; a horrible, booming laugh.

'Bella the bloody sheep! Did you really think she was the one who knocked you unconscious?', Lee continues.

His laugh is now so loud that it causes Otis to recoil.

'Otis what happened to you? Are you okay?', Daphne cries.

Lee immediately stops laughing. His smile vanishes.
'Shut it!', Lee yells.

Daphne quickly turns away. Otis can hear her heavy, rapid breathing.

'You don't speak unless I talk to you. In case you haven't realised, I own you now', Lee says, standing over Daphne.

'So why kill Kiki? You didn't even know him, did you?', Otis says, encouraging Lee to refocus his attention back on him

Lee clearly dislikes these interruptions but cannot resist answering.

'No, I didn't know him at all', Lee replies coldly.

'I don't understand', Otis says.

Lee looks delighted by that statement. He begins to strut around the room, feeling empowered by his captives' helplessness. He gleefully hovers the gun near the head of each prisoner for several seconds, before shouting: BOOM. Otis spots a single tear roll down Daphne's face; it physically pains him. They were all merely playthings to Lee. Jefferson keeps his head down, as if trying his best to hide himself away.

Lee pulls out a pair of handcuffs from his back pocket, and grabs Jefferson roughly by the arm; he twists his wrist until Jefferson lets out a whimper. Lee grins. He proceeds to twist even harder until Jefferson finally screams out. Satisfied that Jefferson is submissive to him, Lee throws a pair of cuffs at him.

'I don't think for one minute you have the guts or strength to do anything, but I don't want you feeling left out', Lee says.

Jefferson looks defeated; terrified.

'Only a weak man feels strong when he has everyone else restrained', Otis says.

Lee storms back over to Otis and pushes the barrel of the gun hard into his chest. He rests his finger on the trigger.

'What did you say?', Lee says. 'Say it again.'

Otis tries to ignore the sharp pain from his ribs being poked so hard.

'I was a detective for a long time, and I know this won't end well for you if you carry on like this', Otis says.

Lee continues to stare, pressing the gun even harder into his chest. He is so close that Otis can smell his breath; it wreaks of stale coffee and smoke. He knows that Lee is calculating his options. Otis wagers he wants to keep them alive a little bit longer, to extend the pleasure he clearly gets from having power over people. Lee holds his position. Otis does not know how much time has passed but it feels like a lifetime. Nothing slows down time like having a loaded gun pressed up against you.

Lee pulls the gun away from him and returns to the doorway and his original pose.

'You wanted to know why I killed Kiki? Ha! You detectives are always looking for some profound reason why someone kills another person. Well, how about that it's fun. Entertaining. Better than TV. It's like hunting. Only with something bigger than a pheasant', Lee says.

Otis looks revolted by his nonchalant manner.

'I can see you disapprove. But what is life but a game. I just choose to play one with higher stakes', Lee says.

'The game will end soon for you, mark my words', Otis says.

Lee sniggers once more; an awful, sinister snigger.

'Thing is old man, you're outnumbered. I didn't do this alone', Lee says.

Otis looks towards Daphne, who looks white as a sheet. Jefferson sits in the corner of the sofa, huddled in a fetal position, his wrists locked together in front of him. Miranda sobs silently, her chin rests on her chest.

'Who helped you?', Otis asks.

'Someone within these very walls', Lee says.

Otis feels Muhsen's phone digging into his side.

'Muhsen?', Otis says.

Lee laughs; a crazy, booming laugh.

'Good guess', he says.

'Muhsen sliced Kiki with one masterful stroke, like a great artist', Lee says, as he heads to the door.

'Muhsen?', Lee calls out. 'Oh Muhsen?'

Otis waits expectantly but he does not appear.

'Oh no, sorry. That can't be what happened, because I killed Muhsen. The poor sap needed putting out of his misery. Better guess again, old man.'

Otis feels sick to his core. He looks at Miranda who appears to be in and out of consciousness. He wonders what happened to them all in the short time he was away.

'What did you do to Muhsen?', Otis asks.

'I squeezed the life out of him. Funny saying that isn't it? Squeezing the life out of someone. It sounds so simple, yet does something so catastrophic', Lee says.

Lee picks up one of the packets of peanuts from the coffee table. He squeezes it in his hand so tightly that the packet pops open, and the peanuts fly everywhere.

'It was as easy as that', Lee says. 'He was gone within minutes of him entering the bedroom. Now that's masterful.'

Lee looks so proud of himself, as he relives the moment in his head.

'You won't get away with this. People will come looking. Not least, they'll wonder why this pub is shut and where the landlady has gone', Otis says.

Lee appears to be losing interest. He begins stroking his gun again. Otis wants to keep him talking; the longer he talks then the more time he has to think of a plan.

'So, humour an old detective would you. How did you play this game? Who else was on your team?', Otis says.

He is unsure if Lee is bluffing about having an accomplice, but it is plausible someone else could be lurking anywhere in the pub. Lee stays silent, still fixated on his gun;

completely consumed by the power it affords him. Otis catches Daphne's eye.

'Did you see anyone else?', Otis mouths silently.

Daphne shakes her head. Otis turns back to look at Lee, who did not detect this little exchange.

'Thing is, what is the point of going to all this trouble if you don't bother sharing how you pulled it off? Seems wasted effort', Otis says dismissively.

Lee's mouth twitches with disdain. Otis can tell he does not want to rise to the bait but he is confident he will.

'What is the point of going to these great lengths, if no one will remember you. No one will know who you are', Otis continues.

'I know what you're doing', Lee says.

He lowers the gun and points it towards Otis. Daphne, Jefferson and Miranda simultaneously let out a weak cry.

'Please don't', Miranda utters, barely able to choke out the words.

Otis remains calm; he chooses to trust his gut. Lee will want to share his story. *Please God let me be right this time*, Otis thinks.

Lee holds the gun steady; no one in the room dares move.

'Well, it only seems fair that my real accomplice joins me to tell the story', Lee says.

He pulls his gun away from Otis again, and reaches into his pocket for a small key. Otis's relief at not being shot is short-lived when he realises what the key is for.

'Come on, your starring role is over. Time to remove the cuffs and be set free', Lee says.

All the hostages look at one another with a rush of suspicion. The accomplice is within this room.

The next few moments play out in super speed. Otis barely has time to process what is happening. Lee reaches towards Daphne's handcuffs.

Otis did not anticipate this; both his mouth and heart drop, as he watches on in dread. It is the last person he wants it to be.

'No!', Otis shouts.

He finds himself losing control of his emotions; a flood of anger crashes through him. Lee watches on in delight.

'Oh dear. Is someone feeling betrayed?', Lee says, with a mocking sad face.

Lee presses his finger and thumb on Daphne's cheeks, preventing her from speaking.

'I'd feel sad to be betrayed by this cutey pie too, but what can I say? She prefers a strong, bad boy', Lee jeers at Otis.

Lee removes his hands, and smiles with glee.

'Only kidding', Lee says, stepping away from Daphne. 'As if I would have her as my accomplice.'

'Fucking hell', Otis cries.

He had never experienced such a rollercoaster of emotion. Daphne looks at him apologetically and fraught with fear; they stare at each other for a moment; their eyes speak a million words.

'Aww. Look at that. You really did not want it to be her, did you?', Lee says, watching Otis. 'Developed a soft spot? Don't worry, I'll make sure to kill her last and give you a front row seat.'

Otis feels a rabid rage ignite inside of him. Daphne shakes her head, urging him to not do anything spontaneous.

'Who would ever want you as their partner?', Daphne cries, unable to suppress her own emotions.

'Wait, what are you doing?', Otis says, fearing Lee will turn his attention back to her.

Lee simply cackles manically. He swoops round behind Miranda and unlocks her handcuffs.

'Thanks, my love', Miranda says to Lee.

Otis, Daphne and Jefferson can do nothing except look on, riddled with alarm and betrayal. All along Miranda had played the innocent landlady, knowing that the body count was piling up; Otis feels more appalled by this than he does by Lee. He had spent several hours with this woman; in her house, accepting her hospitality, even appreciating her kindness to let them stay.

'You lying piece of-'

'Ah, Ah, Ah. Come on, Daphne. No need for that', Miranda says.

Otis likes Daphne's feistiness but not in this situation; he would rather she stays quiet. He tries to shift their attention back to him.

'So, you two are in on all this together? What was it then, a spontaneous or pre-meditated murder? You couldn't have known that train was going to get cancelled', Otis says.

Lee and Miranda exchange a knowing glance.

'Yes, how could we possibly have known, Lee?', Miranda says, with fake confusion.

'Sometimes luck is just on your side. Spur of the moment always makes the show more fun', Lee says.

'Oh, I love a bit of improv', Miranda adds.

Lee smiles and wraps his arm around Miranda's shoulders. Otis has a sinking feeling that there is something to this story yet to be revealed, that is far bigger and more sinister than the murders within these walls.

'Go on then, talk me through it. What happened? Did Lee hover outside and knock on the door and run away? Before finally killing someone. Hardly an elaborate plan', Otis says mockingly.

Miranda and Lee look visibly irritated; they resent anyone questioning their brilliance.

'Can't we just finish that bastard off now? He is doing my head in', Lee asks Miranda aggressively.

She rests a hand on his arm which appears to instantly sooth him. Otis wonders whether Lee, as bolshy as he is, is actually the submissive one.

'It's about setting the scenes. The characters. The drama', Miranda says, giving an admiring glance towards Lee.

'And the misdirection', Lee interjects.

'Come on, tell me how many times you suspected someone else in the group? The sheath, where Jefferson sat. The ID in Daphne's purse. The Dictaphone behind the sideboard. The blood on Miranda's shoe. Muhsen's note. Muhsen's phone. All designed to mess with your head', Miranda says proudly.

Miranda and Lee chuckle with joy and congratulate each other; Otis thinks they are going to take a bow at one point.

'So, did we succeed? Did we screw with your head?', Miranda says.

She moves closer to Otis, staring deep into his eyes. A cold, hard stare enough to unnerve any man.

'What Dictaphone? What blood?', Otis asks.

This only causes the murderers to cackle even more.

'I'll take that as a yes', Miranda says.

This really is all a show for them, Otis thinks. *Nothing more, nothing less.*

'You literally create your own murder mystery to star in', Otis says disapprovingly.

He knows that their finale will involve killing everyone who is left. He needs to think quickly. If he can find a way to get Lee to put down the gun, he may be in with a chance. Otis shifts his strategy. Daphne is staring intently at him; he tries to give a reassuring nod. It is all he can do.

'I don't know. I'm not convinced you two could pull off such an elaborate plan in such a short space of time. You said yourself, luck plays a big part rather than brains', Otis says.

He can see Daphne in the corner of his eye looking horrified that he appears to be hell-bent on goading them. He wants them to feel affronted; he wants them to feel so insulted by his disbelief, that they become pre-occupied with telling him every last detail to prove their intelligence. He needs to buy some time. Right on cue, Miranda and Lee look insulted.

'Well, that's your problem not ours', Miranda says unconvincingly.

Otis laughs, much to their astonishment. It took everything to force that laugh; it is the last thing he felt like doing. Daphne looks at him with equal amazement but is hopeful this is part of some wider plan that will not get them all killed.

Lee runs over to Otis and grabs him by his hair and pulls it violently; Otis bites his lip to suppress crying out from the pain. Once again, Lee holds the gun to Otis's head. Daphne screams. It pierces through Otis's ears. He hates hearing that sound with every fibre of his being.

'I'm going to enjoy killing you, perhaps even more than I enjoyed killing all the others down in the cellar. At least they had the sense to keep their mouths shut', Lee says.

He releases his grip on Otis's hair and walks back to Miranda who rubs his arm like a mother would to an upset child.

'Shh now, don't get yourself worked up. Remember we are here to put on a show, so if he wants a story let's give him a story', Miranda says.

'Yeah alright. I suppose he'll be dead in half an hour anyway', Lee says coolly.

'Oh, I think he'll wish he is dead long before then. The weakness of a good man is that his heart breaks so easily when faced with the acts of pure evil', Miranda says.

A disturbing look creeps across her face. Otis assumes this must be the face of her true self; long gone is the ordinary face of a landlady.

Miranda and Lee take centre stage. Their story begins.

Chapter 10
The Murderer Among Us

'Some are born great, some achieve greatness, and others think they are great.'

Devon, England, 1993:

'I feel different', Lee says, clutching the action figure that had been given to him.
'Different in what way?', the therapist asks.
Lee shrugs, and plays with the toy. The therapist watches Lee tear the limbs from the figure with delight.
'Do you enjoy destroying things?', the therapist asks.
Lee stares at the detached arms and legs in his hands. He shrugs.
'I like playing with things and then destroying them', Lee says flatly.
'Why do you want to destroy them?', the therapist asks.
Lee casually tosses the broken limbs onto the coffee table. The therapist continues to stare at Lee intently but looks a little uncomfortable.
'I saw a cat capture a mouse once. It played with the mouse for ages. It got the mouse to bend to its will. It commanded the creature to run back and forth between its paws. The mouse was so scared that it didn't even realise there was no escape. It just kept running round and round in circles. Then when the cat was done, it killed it with one simple swipe of its claw', Lee says with a glint in his eyes.
The therapist shuffles in his seat.
'Is that something you feel like doing too?', the therapist asks.

Lee grins and stares into the eyes of the therapist.

'Mummy told me to say no', Lee says.

The therapist pauses for a second, his pen poised to write but no ink meets the paper. He looks at the broken action figure, and then back at Lee.

'What would you like to be when you grow up?', the therapist asks.

'An actor', Lee responds with a smile.

'Why an actor?', the therapist asks.

'Because then I can be myself by playing somebody else', Lee says.

Leeds, England, 2003:

Lee sits in the circle along with the other wannabe actors, staring at the instructor stood in the middle giving meaningless lessons. Lee feels empty; bored and unfulfilled. He thought the thrill of being on stage in front of a live audience would help feed his desire for drama, his ache for adrenaline. Getting to star on a stage was proving difficult though.

The teacher instructs everyone to warm their vocal cords. Lee looks around at all the wannabes that fill the room, and feels detached from them all. Each one of them chased the fame and fortune that comes from being an actor, but Lee always felt his need is more primal. More meaningful. He has had enough of these mind-numbing lessons. He gets up from the hard, plastic seat and decides to leave the group for good, unsure where he intends to go next. He feels his options are dwindling by the day.

As he exits the hall, a hand grip his arm firmly; so tightly that it almost hurts him. He turns to find Miranda. Lee stares at her dark eyes, and wild curly hair. She is the only person in the group he could tolerate. There is something different about her. Something magnetising.

'Where are you going?', she asks.

'I just find it a bit shit and pointless in there', Lee says.
Miranda laughs silently.
'Yeah. Well, I only kept coming for you', she says.
She is bold. Fearless. Lee likes it.
'Oh yeah? Why's that?', Lee asks.
'Because I think you're like me. Different. Searching for something more than those lot in there', Miranda says.

Lee feels his mouth smile involuntarily.

'I don't think you want what I want', Lee says, turning away.

'Oh, I wouldn't be so sure. I think you sought out acting for the thrill, but what you really crave is something bigger, something wilder', Miranda says. 'In a world that gives us nothing, why should we conform to its rules?'

Lee turns back to face her.

'If my own mother is uninterested in me, then why are you?', Lee asks.

Miranda detects no sadness in that statement, only bitterness.

'You mean she rejected you for who you are?', Miranda presses.

Lee's face flashes with rage.

'Don't get mad, get even. I know it sounds cliched, but it's probably the wisest advice there is', Miranda says.

'What do you want from me?', Lee asks.

He begins to pull away, uncertain of her true motives and feeling untrusting of anyone but himself.

'I just want us to have some fun', she says, with a sinister grin.

'What kind of fun?', Lee asks.

'Why don't you tell me', Miranda says.

Lee looks her up and down, still unsure if this is some sort of trap.

'It's not a trap', Miranda says.

Lee looks stunned.

'No, I'm not reading your mind', she adds cheekily.

Lee looks even more stunned.

'Okay, you've got me interested', Lee says.

Brighton, England, 2005:

Lee stands on the edge of the stage, soaking in the sight of hundreds of red empty chairs that lay before him.

'Come on, no time to stand around. You need to go and help set up the refreshments stand', a bold-headed man barks at Lee.

Lee ignores him, trying not to let his deep hatred of the man get the better of him. The man persists, and marches over to Lee.

'Daydream about being the star of the show in your own time. Right now, you're just a stagehand, so go and do your job before I fire you', the bald man snarls.

Lee whips around to face the man, his fists clenched, his adrenaline surges. He wants to snap his neck.

'Hello', a woman's voice flows into Lee's ears causing him to lose his focus. He turns to see Miranda stood next to him. The bald man dismissively waves his hand at Lee.

'Just get on with your job, would you?', he says, marching off leaving Miranda and Lee alone.

'You looked like you were about to kill him', Miranda observes.

'I was', Lee says flippantly.

Miranda looks beguiled by this.

'Really?', she says.

'Unfortunately, a beautiful woman distracted me', Lee says, moving closer to Miranda.

She beams. Lee knows she is smitten with him. He likes the fact that his dark side can run free with her.

'I'm glad you didn't kill him. Well, not here anyway. Not like this. If you're going to kill someone, I think you should follow two simple rules', Miranda says.

Lee looks enthralled. He pulls her closer.

'Go on', he says.

'Rule 1: try not to get caught. Rule 2: make it entertaining', she says with a giggle.

Lee stares into her eyes. *Perhaps I'm smitten too,* he wonders as he strokes her slightly protruding belly.

'Entertaining how?', Lee asks.

Miranda breaks free from his embrace, and stands back with her arms outstretched, looking around at the stage.

'You've always wanted to be the star of a show. And you've always wanted to kill. Well, here is your chance to do both, my love', Miranda says with glee.

Lee is mesmerised by this idea. He looks up at the poster for tonight's performance:

Murder on the Orient Express

He joins Miranda at the centre of the stage.

'Our very own murder mysteries', Lee says.

Miranda throws her head back and smiles broadly.

'All the world's a stage, and all the men and women merely players. They have their exits…'

'… and their entrances', Lee interrupts her, and finishes the quote.

Miranda leans against him and shakes her head.

'No, it is only their exits we care about', she says, shaking her finger at him.

Lee smiles with devilish delight.

'I mean, if we can't trust Shakespeare who can we trust?', Miranda says.

Lee wraps his arms around Miranda and looks out into the crowdless theatre.

'Do you remember that night we watched the Merchant of Venice?', Miranda asks.

'How could I forget?', Lee replies.

'They don't write plays like Shakespeare these days', Miranda says sadly.

Lee moves around to face Miranda and takes her hand.

'A stage where every man must play a part, and mine a bad one', Lee says.

'I believe the actual line is "a sad one"', Miranda quips.

'Ah yes, but I think I'm more suited to be bad, don't you?', Lee says with relish.

The bald man returns, red-faced and flustered.

'For goodness' sake, go and sort out that refreshment stand', he shouts.

Lee smiles.

'Of course. Right away', Lee replies.

Miranda looks at him in surprise.

'Why so polite suddenly?', Miranda says.

'Our first show has begun. I'm merely playing my part', Lee says.

He watches the bald man disappear backstage.

'And little does he know that he is already playing his', Lee adds.

Norfolk, England, 4 days ago:

'I hear the Prewett's are leaving for Australia the day after tomorrow', Miranda says.

Lee grunts.

'Not surprising, given The Kings Feet gets zero customers these days. I hear that they plan to go out for six months initially, travel around and then may sell up if they decide to stay out there', Miranda continues.

'Why are you telling me this?', Lee says irritably.

'I hear that they have no family. No kids. No local friends anymore. Hence choosing to travel as they near their twilight years', Miranda says.

Lee looks disinterested.

'My point is, before we also leave this area for good, we may have the makings of another show', Miranda says.

Lee's demeanour suddenly changes. His face lights up with excitement.

'Ah yes. A rundown pub in the middle of nowhere, and a couple isolated. It writes itself', Lee says rubbing his hands together.

He leans down and writes something on a polaroid picture before placing it inside the sleeve of an album.

'There, finished', he says proudly.

Miranda walks over to take a look.

'Perfect, my love', Miranda says.

She stares at the image on the polaroid. A man and his wife lay lifeless on the floor of an unused stable. The words written beneath the image read:

Number 12: The Slaughter in the Stable

'Of course, number 6 was my particular favourite', Miranda says.

She flicks back the sleeves of the album, and points at a different polaroid. Lee looks at it fondly; he studies an image of two wheelie bins. The handwritten caption below reads:

Collection Day

'Ah, the sheer poetic irony of a debt collector being left outside ready for collection', Miranda says gleefully.

'Good ol' days', Lee says.

'You're sounding like an old man', Miranda says, looking disappointed.

'Which was your favourite anyway?', she asks.

Lee closes the album.

'Number 2', Lee replies without hesitation.

'Ah yes, your mother', Miranda says.

Lee locks the small album away in a box disguised as a book, and places it in his rucksack.

'Do you ever feel like it's getting too easy?', Lee asks.

Miranda considers this for a minute.

'Sometimes. Do you?'

'We've got away with every murder so far. No one has ever come knocking on our doors. Either we are too good, or the Police are terrible', Lee says.

'Best not to get too confident. Luck can be as fragile as life and death', Miranda replies.

Lee looks at Miranda, his eyes full of wanting.

'I need more. I need the stakes to be higher', Lee cries.

'How could the stakes be higher?', Miranda says, a little taken aback.

'I need what all directors do. A blockbuster. Bigger cast. Bigger audience', Lee says. His eyes sparkle with madness.

Norfolk, England, Present day:

The storm warning blasts out of the car radio, as Lee drives at speed down the country roads, on his way back from Calnesbury. His eyes glisten with glee; he loves a good storm. He reaches over to the passenger seat and grabs a sausage roll from a carrier bag.

In the distance he spots some lights. As he nears, he realises it is a group of pedestrians huddled together walking in the middle of the road.

Lee slams on the breaks. He looks back at them through the rear-view mirror, and studies them. They look like a group of lost travellers, clinging to phones that are now nothing more than torches. He wagers they will stop at the pub. With a sinister plan hatching in his head, he speeds off down the road.

Lee enters the pub with the carrier bag of snacks.

'Change of plan', he says to Miranda. 'Let's stick around here for another day or two. I think we have another improv opportunity.'

Miranda looks at him, intrigued.

'Oh?'

Lee describes the group of people he has just seen.

'I guess it could be fun. We need to be careful though', Miranda says.

'Don't worry. The pub owners are dead, and they'll never find them down in the cellar. We just need to make sure when they arrive, that they have no option but to stay here', Lee says.

He pulls out the telephone table and unplugs the cord from the wall.

'The storm will help us', Lee says.

'How can you be sure they won't have managed to contact someone for help?', Miranda says, sounding concerned.

Lee looks irritated by the question.

'You'll soon know if they have, when they arrive. I'm guessing not, given they are all walking around in a storm from the direction of the train station', Lee says rather snippily.

'Sounds like I'm taking the leading role in this one', Miranda says arrogantly.

'Hey, don't get too full of yourself. I'll be doing the heavy lifting behind the scenes. You just need to make sure you get everyone in the right places at the right time', Lee instructs.

'This does seem one of our riskier shows. We've never had so many people to cast at once', Miranda says.

'I'm not worried. We're isolated here. The nearest neighbour is going to be me', Lee says. 'And this pub was closed. That's why the owners were off to Australia tomorrow.'

'Well, technically they are down under', Miranda says with a cackle.

Lee does his signature evil snigger.

'Remember, you get them to the right places at the right time. I'll do the rest', Lee reiterates.

'What if one of them does leave, and tries their luck walking to Dillingford', Miranda says.

'Then they will bump into me before they reach anywhere, won't they?', Lee says impatiently.

'Let's go through everything. We don't have much time', Miranda urges.

'And how do we decide who we kill first?', Miranda adds.

'Let's make it simple. Learn their names, and we'll pull them from a hat.'

The pair burst into deranged laughter.

'Let's choose our characters, and get ready for the show of our life', Lee says with excitement. 'Could be the best one of our careers so far.'

Lee rolls up one of his trousers and checks his knife is secured.

'Where have you put our rucksacks?', Miranda asks.

'It's all safely hidden in Calnesbury,' Lee says.

'Oh, one other thing. Let's really screw with their heads. Let's leave a trail of clues that makes every one of them the suspect', Lee says with malice.

'Of course, my love. I wouldn't have it any other way', Miranda says.

'I'll see what I can find in their belongings when they're distracted. Honey, luck really does shine down on us. Listen to that storm brewing outside. What a setting', Lee says, positively beaming with delight.

He heads towards the cellar to grab some of the bottles of drink stored in crates.

'It's a bit of a dump this place, but I think that'll add to the horror they are about to experience', Miranda says, studying the scene around her.

Lee plonks a selection of drinks on the bar.

'We can't be a pub without having a few drinks to offer, Lee says.

Miranda begins setting the scene; she finds some glasses, and stores the drinks away.

'If this goes wrong and we get caught, we will stick to our pact, won't we?', Miranda asks.

Lee chooses to not immediately answer, causing Miranda to pause what she is doing and tap loudly on the countertop with her fingers.

'Lee?', she says loudly.

'Yes, yes. We will stick to our pact', he says.

Lee disappears into the back rooms of the pub, mapping out each nook and cranny so he can plot his hiding places and escape routes. His mind cannot help but sing from the pure happiness of reaching his thirteenth kill. He longed to surpass the body count of all other killers. The only thing that could get in his way is the pact he and Miranda had made. He toyed with the idea of breaking it, but he could never bring himself to be a liar like his mother. An actor, yes. But a liar? He would sooner be put behind bars.

Chapter 11
From Bar to Bars

"We seek out the guilty before we fully know the sin."

As Otis listens to their story, a rising feeling of disgust fill his body. He cannot allow such a vile pair to walk free. They talk with such pride, as they walk the captive audience through their life journey. Otis has the distinct impression that this may be the first time they have had the opportunity to share such truths, outside of their own sadistic union. The casual callousness towards every human life except their own is truly gut wrenching. However, as expected, Lee and Miranda's guard begins to slip as their perverse nostalgia possesses them. Otis waits in eager anticipation; he watches Lee place his gun down as if in slow motion, as Miranda beckons him into a celebratory embrace. Otis prays that they turn their back on the gun, just for a moment, because then he may be in with a chance. He knows Daphne is staring at him, but he remains focussed. His mouth turns dry, his pulse becomes erratic. He stares intensely, willing his plan into action.

The opportunity finally arrives. The duo come to the end of their storytelling, and turn to congratulate each other once again on their successes. Lee turns his back on the gun, leaving it unattended for a few seconds. It is enough time for Otis to put his scheme in motion. He pulls free of his handcuffs and lunges for the gun. Rapidly straightening up, he rests his hand on the trigger ready to pull it. Otis blocks out the pain that this rapid movement has inflicted on his battered back. Lee spins around ready to attack but immediately backs away spotting Otis's trigger-ready finger, which is as steady as a ship on still waters. Lee looks furious, his nostrils flare and his eyes are ready to pop; resembling a wild restrained animal, lusting at its prey beyond its reach.

'Word of advice, never ask a hostage to lock their own handcuffs. Idiot', Otis says with an air of satisfaction.

Daphne feels like she is going to pass out, there is only so much real-life drama she can handle; she longs to feel the pages of her books between her fingers, instead of the metal cuffs wrapped around her wrists. Jefferson looks like he has already passed out.

'So, what's the plan then, old man?', Lee says, raising his hands up in an attempt to appear unbothered.

Otis knows that he is bothered though. He can see the growing fury in Lee's eyes. Otis wonders how long it has been since Lee has felt this out of control.

'Drop the key to the cuffs on the floor', Otis says.

Lee resists.

'Now', Otis demands.

Otis can tell Lee loathes taking instructions; his eyes, mouth and nose pulsate with rage. Lee desperately wants to lunge at Otis. Miranda nudges Lee to throw the key on the floor. Lee curses at her before reluctantly pulling the key out of his pocket. Otis knows he has to be ready to pull the trigger; he tightens his grip. Lee furiously throws the key on the floor, it bounces towards Daphne. Otis does not look, he continues to match Lee's hard stare.

'You have your precious key. Now what, old man?', Lee says.

'Now drag your sorry arse out that door and towards the cellar. Now!', Otis shouts.

He does not even glance at Daphne or Jefferson; even if he looks away for a second, he knows Lee will strike. Daphne watches on feeling helpless, as Otis escorts them out of the room. She bounces over towards Jefferson on the other end of the sofa and gives him a whack with her elbow. Jefferson looks startled.

'Come on Jefferson. I need you! We need to get down to those keys, and help Otis', she cries.

Jefferson looks spaced out, his eyes still red from crying. He is unsure what to do, and resembles a schoolboy who is afraid of breaking the rules.

'Come on, Jefferson! Pull yourself together. I can't do this without you', she says.

Jefferson remains unresponsive. Daphne throws her head back against the headrest; she groans with frustration.

'Fine, I'll have to see what I can do on my own', she mutters.

Jefferson watches Daphne, he pulls on his handcuffs feebly.

'How are we meant to get ourselves free?', Jefferson says.

'With a little bit of imagination', Daphne replies.

She manages to grab the key with her fingers.

Otis rounds the corner to the cellar and encourages Lee and Miranda to enter with a few firm nudges on their back, using the barrel of the gun. Lee and Miranda sluggishly pass through the cellar doorway; Otis knows they are trying to work out how to overpower him before he can pull the trigger. They turn around to face Otis, with unnerving smirks on their faces.

'Stay where you are', Otis demands.

Lee licks his lips and laughs, looking increasingly unhinged.

'I don't think you'll pull that trigger. You're not a killer', Lee says.

'I've been a lead detective and cop for decades. Do you really think I won't use a gun?', Otis replies.

Otis quickly shuts the door, but is caught out by a bolt of pain shooting down his spine. Before he has time to lock it Lee and Miranda storm forward causing the door to burst open, and knocking Otis backwards onto the floor. He loses grip of the gun which goes flying towards the other side of the pub seating area. Before he can react, Otis sees Lee running towards him, ready to pounce on top of him and exact his revenge. Lee's hands wrap around Otis's neck; they are hot and sweaty. Otis's head feels ready to burst as it slowly suffocates.

BANG.

A shriek rings out. Lee jumps off Otis; everyone turns to look at who pulled the trigger. Daphne is stood holding the gun, her face overcome with shock as she stares at the hole in the wall she made. She had never fired a gun before; her shoulder throbs from the throwback but she does not dare let on. Otis scrambles to his feet.

'Consider that a warning shot', she says, mustering the toughest sounding voice she can, unintentionally sounding cockney.

Lee snorts looking unconvinced; he takes a few steps towards her. Daphne holds the gun high and points it at him. Everyone looks at her, trying to gauge her next move.

'I mean it. I'm on the edge. I've had enough', she screams.

'No', Miranda utters quietly to Lee, fearing he will do something that will get him killed.

Lee obeys and takes a few steps back, returning to Miranda.

Otis hurries over to take control of the gun again. Daphne willingly hands it over.

'Very gangster', he whispers to her, with a brief look of gratitude.

'Right, you two, let's try this again. Get in the cellar', Otis says to an increasingly petulant looking Lee and Miranda.

They both fail to move.

'Let's not do this again. It's getting boring now. Get in there now', Otis says.

This time it is his rage that is rising; he is feeling increasingly exhausted and tries to muster the last bit of strength he has. His throat feels bruised; it still feels like he has Lee's fingers digging into his skin.

Lee and Miranda reluctantly head into the cellar once more. Otis suspects they will try to escape again.

'I'd rather you just shoot us to be honest', Lee says, standing on the brink of entering the cellar.

Miranda does not look impressed with him.

'What are you talking about?', she cries.

'Well, would you rather be dead or be sat in jail?', Lee says.

'I'd rather not be dead, you moron', Miranda snaps.

She pulls him towards her, into the cellar.

Otis is almost amused by the spectacle of them having such an insane squabble, in an even more insane situation.

'You think you've won, old man. But you haven't. Do you want to know why', Lee says.

Otis does not like how happy he looks all of a sudden.

Miranda slaps Lee on the arm.

'Shut it. Remember the pact', she says angrily.

Lee goes quiet. Daphne moves closer to Otis.

'Be ready. Be quick. Use all your strength to hold the door shut' Otis says quietly to Daphne.

'Don't fear, I am here to help', Jefferson declares.

His arrogant tone appears to be making a comeback.

'How long have you been there?', Daphne asks.

'Long enough to see you need an extra pair of hands', he replies.

'Wait, what is that?', Daphne shouts, as she snatches something from Jefferson's hand so quickly that he has no time to stop her.

She holds up a large knife. Daphne stares wide eyed at Jefferson. Otis fleetingly stares at the knife but maintains his position.

'What are you playing at?', Otis asks.

Jefferson looks alarmed.

'Why would I come in here with two murderers and not be armed? I grabbed it from the kitchen as soon as I heard the gun go off', he says.

Otis's eyes dart between Lee, Miranda and Jefferson.

Lee's grin fades: both he and Miranda begin to look defeated. Perhaps realising they are finally outnumbered, Otis surmises.

'For God's sake, I just wanted to protect myself. I heard the kafuffle taking place; wouldn't you have grabbed something before coming in?', Jefferson says.

Daphne looks at Otis.

'He doesn't seem to have anything else on him', she says with a shrug of the shoulder.

'Fine', Otis says. 'Help Daphne shut the door. We don't want any more bloodshed.'

'Um… perhaps you are better off helping with the door. You're much stronger than me', Jefferson says, backing away from Lee and Miranda.

'Bloody hell, Jefferson. Just do it! I will be the one to stand here with my finger on the trigger. Any funny business, I won't hesitate to pull it. I never have before', Otis says, glowering at the two murderers.

Jefferson looks subdued once more.

'You may think you have won, but mark my words there is a sequel coming', Lee calls out.

His eyes dig deep into Otis.

'Lock them away', Otis says, feeling sick of the sight of them.

Jefferson walks over to the door with Daphne, and they quickly slam it shut. Daphne desperately tries not to fumble as she locks it as quickly as she can. She immediately runs over to Otis and hands him the key.

'I feel safer if you have this', she says.

Otis wants to ask her how she is, but it seems such a foolish question to ask.

'Good job I came along. You couldn't have held that door shut on your own', Jefferson says.

Otis and Daphne exchange a bemused look.

'You've suddenly woken up' Daphne says, eyeing Jefferson with curiosity.

He looks sheepish, almost embarrassed.

'Yeah, well I thought I was a goner back in there', Jefferson says, pointing in the direction of the living room.

'Right, let's finally get the bloody police here', Otis declares.

'Aren't you going to put that down now?', Jefferson says, staring nervously at the gun.

'Oh, I don't think so. I want to be ready in case of anymore surprises', Otis replies.

Jefferson raises an eyebrow.

'You think there will be more surprises?', he asks.

'After the last twenty-four hours I think it's best to be ready for anything', Otis replies.

Daphne rushes around to the side of the bar where the phone is. Pulling the table out, she spots the hanging cord and plugs it back in.

'If only I'd checked whether it was plugged in in the first place', Daphne says, slapping her forehead with her palm.

Jefferson looks unamused. Otis looks the opposite.

'Hindsight is-'

'a bitch', Daphne says, finishing Otis's sentence.

'Indeed', Otis says.

She dials the three-digit number. Who knew three numbers could bring such elation and relief. After a frantic call trying to explain the situation, Daphne puts down the receiver and looks towards Otis with a huge sense of a weight lifting from her.

'Help is finally on its way', she says, leaning back against the wall with a large exhale of breath.

'Good. We'll be safe now', Otis says.

'That's what you think', Daphne says. 'Shame you never spotted that I'm actually their third accomplice.'

Otis gawps at her. All the tension that had just been released from his body comes hurtling back in a tornado of panic. Jefferson looks like a ghost, and nearly falls off the bar stool.

'What the hell?', Jefferson exclaims.

'Sorry, sorry. I'm joking. I have an awful habit of making the most inappropriate jokes in very awkward situations', Daphne says, looking regretful.

'Calling this whole thing an *awkward situation* is a bit of an understatement', Otis says, wiping a bead of sweat from his forehead.

Jefferson buries his face in his hands, mumbling something incoherently. Daphne apologises again, feeling silly at her attempt at joviality in such a serious situation.

'I can't wait to sit down and have a stiff drink', Otis says.

'Obviously at a different pub', he adds dryly.

He remains stood to attention, gun at the ready. Jefferson watches him carefully, with a hint of distrust.

The wait is unbearable. No one dares talk; it is unnervingly quiet. The trapped murderers make no sound. Jefferson keeps eyeing the cellar door nervously; he rocks back and forth.

'They're locked away, I doubt they are going to be able to break out surely', Jefferson says.

Otis does not respond. He waits patiently for the sound of the calvary arriving.

'How do we know the police aren't going to accuse us? Do you think they'll just confess? It's our word against theirs' Jefferson continues. His nerves grow as the time ticks by.

Otis maintains his grip on the gun but perches on the edge of the table near Jefferson, who in turn gives another resentful glance at the weapon.

'I'm only hanging onto this as a precaution. Best to never leave something like this unattended in these circumstances. Anyway, yes, the police will have questions for us. And even if those two in there don't confess, I highly doubt they've left no trail of evidence', Otis says.

'I just can't believe this is all real', Daphne says, staring at the now vacated spot on the floor where Kiki had been. 'I suppose it will hit me properly the moment I get back to my own home.'

'Fortunately, serial killers are a minority. You stumbling into this mess is the equivalent of winning the lottery, in terms of the odds. Obviously without the huge joy of cash at the end', Otis replies.

Otis looks over at the area by the front door.

'Why did they move Kiki's body anyway?', he asks.

Daphne recoils as she recalls what happened.

'They were doing something down in the cellar, with the bodies. It was like they were creating an artistic display or something', Daphne says.

She looks mortified, as the realisation of how truly disturbed Lee and Miranda are dawns on her. Otis does not know what to say in response. He feels as sick and appalled as she does.

'I'm sorry I left you', Otis says.

A lump forms in his throat; a clump of guilt almost chokes him. He grows tired of letting people down.

'They're here', Daphne screams, much louder than she intended.

Otis readies the gun, completely caught off guard by Daphne's hysteria. He turns his head towards the windows and sees a flash of blue.

Finally, the Calvary is here, he thinks.

Detective Langley's excitement at being called to a multiple homicide almost borders on being distasteful. Otis can only assume this is his first one. Or, at the very least, a very rare occurrence in his area. He marches around giving orders, and declares to anyone who listens that he, and he alone, is the person in charge.

Otis watches on, as Miranda and Lee are escorted out by officers. The perpetrators' faces look blank, void of emotion; they stare at Jefferson and Daphne as they pass by. Otis watches Jefferson and Daphne immediately look tense. Daphne tries to meet their eyes not wishing to give them any further domination over her, but she eventually turns away. Jefferson manages to hold his gaze.

Whilst Langley is finding this exhilarating, Otis is finding it rather monotonous. He gives his alibi once again, along with Daphne and Jefferson. They all retrace their steps over the last twenty-four hours. It is like reliving a nightmare over and over.

Daphne walks over and joins Otis, who is stood outside the pub near a flurry of police vehicles. She leans into him a little.

'Are you okay?', he says.

'Do you think we can go home now?', she asks hopefully.

'I suspect not. We'll have to go to the station with them, give our statements formally on record', he replies.

He feels Daphne's body quiver, as the bulging body bags are carried from the pub.

'Four people. I can't believe it', Daphne says quietly, shaking her head.

'They think the real pub owners have been down there a couple of days. We were just an unexpected but welcome addition to their killing spree here', Otis says.

He looks up thoughtfully at the old stone building, wondering what kind of ordeal its owners went through. His soul feels heavy; there has been too much darkness lately.

'How's Jefferson doing?', Otis asks.

'Quiet. Think his bravado of yesterday has started to wash away. Not even he can make quips about a situation like this', Daphne says.

'I don't think I'll ever get used to meeting people like Lee and Miranda; so empty of humanity, yet so good at mirroring it', Otis reflects.

Daphne notices the look of guilt that fills his eyes.

'You couldn't have known they were behind all this. Besides, it's better to go through life trying to think the best of people rather than suspect the worst. I'm sure it would change who you are if all you could see was the bad', Daphne says.

Otis hears the words but saves them for later, unable to process them right now.

'Ah, there you are', Detective Langley says, striding towards them. 'What a nasty business this is. The press are going to have a field day.'

Langley stands alongside them, hands in his pockets and legs apart, watching the scene before him like a commander on a ship.

'Good job', Langley randomly shouts to officers as they pass by. Otis wonders if this is all for show, based on the surprised expressions that greet his shouts of praise.

'There's bound to be dozens, perhaps hundreds more' Langley says.

'More what?', Otis asks.

'Bodies', Langley says apathetically.

Daphne is unsettled by this statement; she looks to Otis for assurance, but he is unable to offer much. Sadly, he thinks that Langley could be right.

'You three, go with my officers and I will see you back at the station. We'll try not to keep you much longer. They've confessed to everything', Langley says.

Otis looks surprised.

'They have?', he asks.

'Yes. Why so surprised? I suspect they saw I meant business and knew they had no way out', Langley says.

Otis resists the urge to roll his eyes.

'I'm just surprised they confessed so quickly', Otis says.

Langley looks a little annoyed at Otis's lack of appreciation.

'Well, they had already confessed everything to you', Langley says shortly.

Langley walks off back to his car; Otis knows he is already thinking how he can use this case to get himself a promotion. He had met many people like him in the Force. Daphne suddenly wraps her arm around his, all thoughts of murder and police politics drain from his brain. The only thing Otis can think about is the fact Daphne has her arm in his. His pulse quickens. He feels like a teenage idiot. *Get a grip of yourself,* he thinks.

'Do you know what I really want?', Daphne asks.

Otis stares at her wide eyed.

'A great, big-achoo!'

Daphne's sneeze makes Otis physically jump.

'Coffee', she continues.

'Sorry. I guess the chilly, damp air is getting to me', she adds.

Otis smiles awkwardly.

'Why are you surprised they confessed anyway?', Daphne asks.

'I don't know really. It all just seems too easy. Anti-climactic, dare I say it', Otis says.

'I'm not surprised they did. Given how proud they are of who they are, and what they've done over the years. They don't strike me as the kind of people who would find any appeal in acting all innocent at this stage', Daphne says.

Otis contemplates her words.

'Acting is what they do best', he says.

'But there's the messed up acting they did to lull victims into their narrative, and then there is denying they did all of these acts of evil they are so proud of. People like that get little joy from the latter I reckon', Daphne says.

'Very true. You'd make a good detective', he says.

'Nah. I could never do things by the book', she says.

Otis laughs.

Chapter 12
End Scene

"The last chapter is often just the beginning."

Daphne takes a biscuit and dunks it in her tea.
'Oh blast', she says.
She pulls out the biscuit to find half of it missing. Otis watches on in amusement.
'There's an art to it', he says.
"Yes, it involves not getting distracted mid-dunk', she replies.

She proceeds to shove the remaining half in her mouth; her cheeks puff out like a squirrel storing its food. Otis wonders if he will ever see her again, once she boards her train back home.

'It feels so liberating to be back out in the hustle and bustle of a town. I know it was only 24 hours; but it was 24 hours of hell and murder', Daphne says.

Two days had passed since they escaped their brush with evil. She looks around the busy train station of Hammersly, like a kid seeing it for the first time. The place swarms with people; families, commuters, tourists. A mishmash of life runs through its veins. The grand, golden clock tower rings out a jaunty tune signalling noon has arrived. Daphne's train is due in fifteen minutes. Otis takes a swig of his coffee. For some reason his outlook on the world has shifted. He had become consumed only by vengeance of late, but now something else also occupied his mind.

'Did you ever have a sense who the murderer might be?', Daphne asks.

Otis sighs heavily; he looks downcast.

'Honestly? I am disappointed in myself. I knew the clues were there, but my mind felt too congested to decipher them. Several months ago, it may have been a different story', Otis says.

'Perhaps you're being too hard on yourself. We never truly know who walks among us', Daphne reflects.

'I guess that's true. Still, I feel that I lost a piece of myself during my last case that I've not managed to replace', Otis says. 'It makes me wonder what else I missed', he adds thoughtfully.

Daphne gives him a concerned look; she wonders what is really going on inside that brain of his. He feels instant regret at letting his wall down, and is not even sure why he did. He turns away from her, pretending to read the arrivals board; hoping that she does not pursue the topic further, yet also secretly feeling better from talking about it. It is a confusing feeling to him.

'My money had been on Jefferson for a while. I wasn't sure how much of that was because he annoyed me, mind you', Daphne says.

The edges of Otis's lips turn up a little, as he listens.

'There was just something about him, like he had no warmth. You know?', Daphne continues.

'I know what you mean. Perhaps he had become so used to playing a character on social media, he forgot who he really is', Otis says.

'That's very insightful', Daphne replies.

She takes a bite out of another biscuit; Otis can see her mind whirring.

'Then I soon shifted my suspicions onto Miranda. Although, I kept doubting that someone who would spend over an hour rescuing a sheep would be a serial killer', Daphne says.

She shakes her head and laughs at the absurdity of it all. Otis recalls Miranda's sheep escapade; he is slightly impressed that Daphne's recalls such details.

'It wouldn't surprise me if she chose a story about rescuing an animal deliberately. You know what they say, psychopaths harm animals. So, she probably was trying to be the opposite', Otis says.

Daphne stares up at the ceiling thinking about his theory, she had never thought about it like that.

'The whole thing is such a tragic nonsense. They literally acted as if it was some West End theatre performance. I always thought murderers would have some more profound meaning for being, well, evil', she says.

Otis knows how she is feeling. He had a similar conversation when he first joined the homicide squad. He watches Daphne stir her tea gently, observing how remarkably she has coped with such a traumatic event.

'At least they are behind bars, for good I hope', she adds.

'Indeed', Otis says.

The base of his back still throbs, acting as a continual reminder of his failed excursion to get help. He feels surprisingly grateful to not be the lead investigator for the case.

'So, are you going to attend to the mysterious unfinished business you had?', Daphne asks.

Otis watches a man sprint for a train; despite his best efforts he misses it. The man proceeds to fly into a fit of despair; he throws his bag on the floor. Otis tilts his head to the side, wondering if the path he himself has chosen is the right one.

'About a year ago, I was asked to look over a case where a drunk driver had hit two people and killed them. The crux of the story is that I deduced the alleged passenger had in fact been the driver. Not only that, but it had also been a deliberate act. Pre-meditated murder', Otis says.

Daphne puts her final biscuit back down, her attention now solely on Otis.

'Go on', she says.

'The two people killed were a fellow police officer and his wife. They had a young daughter. I promised that daughter that the man who took her parents from her would be put away. Except, he wasn't. The jury felt my evidence was not sufficient', Otis says, his voice cracks.

Daphne can see how raw this still is for him.

'Why did he target her parents?', Daphne asks.

'The police officer arrested his son for drug offences.'

Daphne waits, expecting more.

'That's it? The officer arrests his son and so he kills him?', Daphne says.

'That's all it took, yes. You see, they think they are above the law; they don't accept any authority except for their own. I don't think they'll stop trying to bring people like that officer down, until the world moulds to their vision', Otis says solemnly.

'The officer was my cousin. A really decent man, who loved his family', Otis adds.

Daphne leans across the table and places her hand on his arm. Otis tries to act casual, like he has not noticed. He appreciates the gesture very much though.

'I quit the police. I was so full of rage that, despite my best efforts, the man walked away scot-free. I felt the only way for him to receive justice would be if I gave it to him personally', Otis says, looking a little ashamed.

Daphne sits back in her chair, removing her hand from his arm. She considers what Otis said. Otis feels sure that she will judge him harshly, and rightly so he thinks.

'I get it', Daphne says. 'I mean, I don't think you should chase after this deranged man like a vigilante. But I get why you feel like you need to.'

Otis feels a sense of relief, like a tiny fragment of the load he has carried is lifting. Her words warm him in a way he has never felt. Daphne glances at the time; her train will be here shortly. For once she actually wishes the train is running late.

'Could you go back to the police?', she asks.

Otis dismisses this idea instantly.

'No. It's not the same for me anymore. Hard to explain, but it doesn't feel like I belong there. I wish I could still help people though, solve cases. I do miss that', he says.

Otis mindlessly turns his cup around in circles on the table; still torn between his resistance to talk, and his need to get things off his chest.

'I still don't think I can fully let it go, and just let him get away with what he did', he adds.

He turns his cup a little too vigorously and some coffee spills. Daphne reaches into her bag to pull out a tissue; she feels her mystery book knock into her hand. She pulls the book out and stares at it.

'You know, this book is about a private investigator. Perhaps that's something to consider, becoming a private investigator I mean', she says. 'And I could help.'

Otis raises his eyebrows sceptically.

'No, think about it. You can help people who feel they have nowhere else to turn. And you can also do a bit of digging on that man; a person like that is bound to have a lot of skeletons in his closet. You may not be able to nail him for what he did to your cousin, but perhaps you can nail him for something else', Daphne says.

The words tumble out of her mouth in a stream of excitement. Otis needs a moment to replay each one in his head. The more he mulls over her idea, the more tempted he is by it.

Daphne's train hisses into the station. She looks disappointed by its arrival.

'Well, what do you think?', she says.

'I think it will be a hard slog, especially in the beginning', Otis replies.

Daphne looks slightly dejected, but she smiles and nods sympathetically.

'Let's do it', Otis says.

Daphne grins in astonishment. She tosses the book in a nearby bin. Otis looks confused.

'Well, I won't be needing that anymore', she declares.

The symbolic gesture soon ended, as she quickly retrieved the book back out of the bin.

'I'll take it to a charity shop', she says.

Pulling out a pen and notepad from her bag, she begins making notes.

'What about your train?', he asks.

"I found something better to do', she says.

Otis has no idea what he has got himself into, but he liked the energy she was bringing to his life. He gets up and goes to order them two more drinks.

Otis returns with two piping hot coffees, just as Daphne's train chugs back out of sight.

'There is one thing though, that you may need to work on', Otis says, taking his seat.

Daphne looks worried.

'What?', she asks.

Otis adopts a deliberately sombre face.

'Your penchant for making jokes at inappropriate moments', Otis says.

Daphne looks embarrassed; Otis suppresses a laugh.

'If it's any comfort, that trait of mine irks me as much as it does everyone else', she says.

'I just don't want you joking you're the guilty party during one of our investigations', he says, with a sparkle of whimsy in his eyes.

Our investigations. I like that, he thinks.

'Oh my gosh', Daphne cries, looking up suddenly from her scribbled notes. 'Isn't that Jefferson?'

Otis turns and spots the tall lanky figure of Jefferson heading towards them.

'I thought that was you two', he says, pulling up a chair with no invitation.

'Surprised you aren't a zillion miles from here after what happened', Jefferson says.

'Likewise', Daphne replies.

Jefferson appears to have a different air about him; the arrogance that seeped from him seems to have been diluted by a lighter, more jovial tone.

'What are your plans then?', Otis asks.

Jefferson points towards a rucksack by his feet.

'I just feel like travelling around, seeing where the road takes me', he replies.

'Really?', Daphne says, sounding surprised.

'Yeah, well, the way I see it is, if I survived that ordeal then I can survive most things', Jefferson replies. 'Besides, I've gone off Hammersley now.'

They all go quiet; no one knows quite what to talk about next. Otis hopes Jefferson will make a move soon. He had been enjoying listening to Daphne's ambitious plans for their future venture and wanted to get back to them.

'I woke up thinking about Kiki and Muhsen', Jefferson continues. 'How one minute they were on a train with plans, and the next minute, poof, they are gone. Robbed of their life.'

Daphne sets her pen down. Otis notices her lip vibrate.

'I liked Kiki. He seemed a bit of a free spirit. He mentioned to me his family had died, I never found out what happened', Daphne says sadly.

Jefferson reaches for his phone and begins to search the internet.

'What are you looking for?', Daphne asks, intrigued.

'Well, all I've got to go on is that he was called Kiki and wrote poems', Jefferson says, tapping away on his phone.

Otis and Daphne watch and wait, wondering if Jefferson will find out anything more about him.

'Aha! Isn't the internet amazing sometimes', Jefferson declares triumphantly. 'Kiki Jones: Poems from a Poisoned Heart.'

Daphne rolls her eyes towards Otis.

'A poisoned heart? Sounds a bit darker than I was expecting', she says.

'I can read the first few pages for free', Jefferson says scrolling through the screen.

'Can I see?', Daphne asks eagerly.

She takes the phone and swipes up to the dedication page. It reads:

To my family, whom I never met.

Daphne's eyes well with water.

'Gosh he really does come across as someone who suffered a lot of heartache', she says.

Otis disliked seeing her upset.

'We can find out more about his family. Perhaps it could be the first trial investigation', Otis says softly.

Daphne knows he is trying to lessen her sadness; she is grateful for the gesture.

'Perhaps we should find out more about Muhsen too. It seems unfair to purely label him as merely an ill-tempered young man. I'm sure there's more to his story too', she says.

Jefferson looks a little lost in the conversation.

'Erm... well, look here. There is a brief biography of the author', Jefferson says.

'Oh, read it', Daphne says with anticipation.

Jefferson clears his throat.

'Okay, well it says: Kiki Jones first started writing poetry at the age of 10. His poems were a way to escape the real world, which had been unkind to him from a young age. Abandoned by his mother, and passed around multiple foster families, he never managed to find a place to call home until he turned 14. A foster family adopted him permanently, and Kiki described this as the happiest time of his life. Sadly, his time with his newfound family was cut tragically short when his adoptive parents were killed in a car accident on his 15th birthday.'

'That's so sad', Daphne says, bringing a tissue up to her eye.

'Yeah, talk about bad luck following you around', Jefferson says.

'I think we've had enough sadness over the last few days', Otis says, eager to change the subject to something more optimistic.

Jefferson puts his phone away.

'What are your plans then? Sounds like you have made joint ones', Jefferson asks.

Otis and Daphne avert their eyes from each other, feeling awkward but unsure why.

'We were just talking about some possible business opportunities', Daphne says.

'And we probably should make a move actually', Otis says, keen to hurry this impromptu reunion with Jefferson along.

Otis and Daphne get up to leave.

'I'll go settle the bill', Otis says to Daphne.

Jefferson steps ahead of him, and raises his hand up in front of him.

'No, let me get this', Jefferson insists.

Otis and Daphne look pleasantly surprised.

'Well, you did get us out of there', Jefferson adds. 'And I don't have many people in my life to treat.'

Otis does not know how to respond to this, but he senses Daphne's stance towards Jefferson softening by the minute.

'Do you need dropping somewhere? Otis has a rental car', Daphne says.

Daphne suddenly looks flustered.

'I mean, not that it's my place to offer up Otis to drive you anywhere', she adds hastily.

Otis rolls his eyes comically at her. He then spots Jefferson's puppy-like eyes staring across at him. *Damn it,* Otis thinks.

'Yeah, it's fine. If you need a lift somewhere nearby then happy to take you', Otis says.

Daphne gives him a gentle nudge to say thank you. Otis is not over the moon about being Jefferson's chauffeur, but he knows Daphne means well. After everything they have been through, ensuring everyone gets safely on their way is probably the most appropriate ending, Otis concludes.

'That would be so great thank you', Jefferson says enthusiastically. 'I'll go pay and catch you up.'

'Sure, okay. We'll be out the front by the North entrance', Otis says.

They head out towards the exit, leaving Jefferson in the café.

Daphne leans into Otis as they walk.

'I just feel a bit sorry for him', Daphne says.

As Jefferson waits at the till to pay, a waitress taps him on the back.

'Sorry lovey, I was just clearing that table. You were sat there, weren't you?', she says.

Jefferson looks over and nods.

'It's just that the lady you were with seems to have left her bag there', she says.

'Oh no problem, I'm catching up with them now. I'll take it with me', he says.

The waitress thanks him, before returning to the table to finish clearing the tray. She picks up the bag and places it on the table; she spots something flash inside of it. It appears to be a piece of metal reflecting the bright light above. The waitress looks a little startled upon realising that it is a knife inside. Unsure what to make of it, she hurries away to the kitchen with the dirty dishes.

Jefferson strides back over and collects the bag. Once out of sight of the café he opens it and glances inside. His knife is still there. He throws his wallet back in, and pushes the knife into one of the side pockets; there is something else inside preventing the knife from going down any further. Reaching in, he pulls out a single polaroid picture with a handwritten caption scribbled across on the bottom that says:

The stars of the show

The image above the caption is of a younger looking Jefferson, Lee and Miranda. He looks at the picture for a moment before hiding it away again. Sometimes he wishes he had never been on that train and on the phone to Lee when it got diverted. Lee's hunger for the next thrill was always at its peak after a recent kill, and he was unable to resist taking advantage of such an unusual opportunity. Everything was handed to Lee on a plate. He was already near the bus depot in Calnesbury; delaying the bus had been a breeze. From that point, Lee felt nothing could go wrong for them. Even Jefferson had brief moments of feeling invincible. Although Jefferson loathed playing the part of the shallow, annoying influencer. Now he finds himself stuck with the irritating alter-ego for longer than he cared. Swinging his bag over his shoulder, he heads out to find Otis and Daphne.

Daphne's mind is still pre-occupied with Kiki. She leans against the car, reflecting on the name of his poetry book.

'You've got one of those modern phones that connects to the internet, haven't you?', she says.

"Oh yes, I have all mod cons', Otis replies.

He pulls the phone from his pocket.

'You want to read his poems, don't you?', Otis says.
Daphne looks flabbergasted.
'How on earth did you guess?'
Otis grins.
'I was a detective, remember', he says.

Daphne puts her bag down on the floor, and takes the phone from him, unsure how much she liked the fact that he was able to read her so accurately.

'Let's read poem one', she says. 'It's called "Wolves".'

The wolves will come out tonight
To hunt, to taunt, to kill their prey
The wolves will come out tonight
To us its death, to them its play

The wolves will come out tonight
Seeking those outside the pack
The wolves will come out tonight
They stab, stab, stab me in the back

The wolves will come out tonight
Watch as they shed their sheeplike skin
The wolves will come out tonight
You best hope and pray you blend in

The wolves are done for tonight
A sea of bloodshed in their wake
The wolves are done, for tonight
Help us for humanity's sake

The wolves are among us, tonight

Daphne lowers the phone slowly, she feels slightly uneasy.

'His poems are a little darker than I thought they would be for some reason', Otis says.

Daphne hands the phone back to him, deep in thought.

'I feel like there was much to know about Kiki. Quite an apt poem when you think about it', she says.

'How do you mean?'

'Well, it almost feels like he's talking to us from beyond the grave. There's something eery about it', she says.

Otis watches Daphne: he knows she is reciting the poem in her head. She spots Otis studying her.

'Perhaps we should move on to lighter things. What could our business be called?'. Daphne says.

'What's your surname?', Otis asks.

'Fear. Daphne Fear.'

Otis smiles widely and begins to laugh.

'What is it?', Daphne says. 'That's a proper surname.'

Otis wipes his eyes, as his laughter draws a tear.

'I know, I'm sorry. It's just if we use both our surnames it would be called Hurt and Fear Investigators.'

'I think you find that funnier than I do. I think it's a great name', she says.

Jefferson spots Otis and Daphne in the distance, he watches them share a joke together. They seem so content in each other's company. *Just like I used to be with my family,* he thinks. Jefferson feels an emptiness without Lee and Miranda by his side; their travelling theatre company is over. The need for retribution brewed inside of him; he wished he could have fought to the death with Otis, and done more than merely watch as they got locked away. That was not the deal though; Miranda always hammered into him that revenge must always come first. Their sacred pact had been, if ever they got caught, one person would always be left to escape: a seemingly innocent bystander. An escapee to ensure that whoever captured them would pay a price for it. An escapee to ensure that their little gang always had the last laugh.

Otis and Daphne spot him, and call him over. *Wish I'd picked a different name,* Jefferson thinks. The name and the whole character of Jefferson is starting to grate. He beams and waves back. He strolls across the road towards them, and re-enters the stage.

'Let's get going. I've had enough of train stations, I don't know about you', Otis says.

They all pile into the car. Daphne sinks back into the seat, feeling grateful to be heading for a new adventure with a newfound friend. Feeling unusually spontaneous, Otis scrolls through the radio and cranks up the volume upon hearing one of his favourite songs: the soothing voice of The Eagles flows through the car.

"You can check out anytime you like, but you can never leave…"

Jefferson sits in the back, planning his next scene. *It's show time,* he thinks.

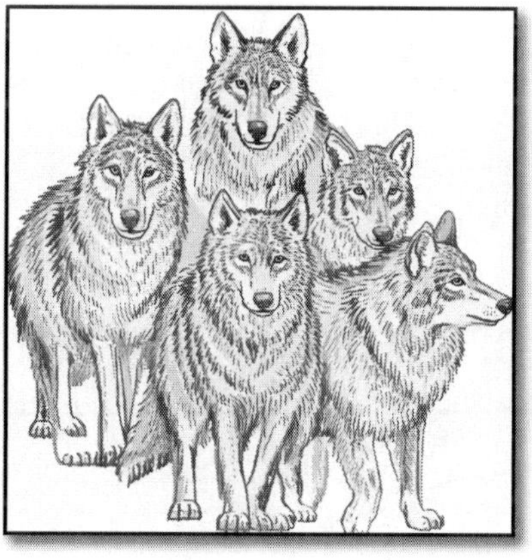

Manufactured by Amazon.ca
Acheson, AB